MOONSHADOW

MOONSHADOW

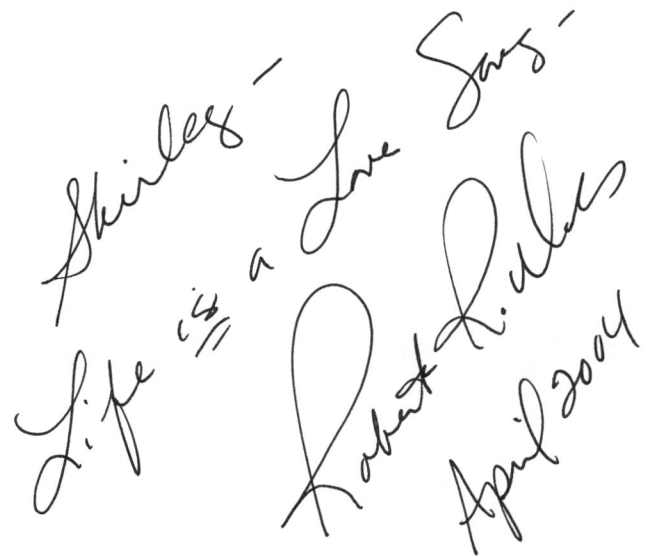

Roberta Rosenfield Wells

Copyright © 2000 by Roberta Rosenfield Wells.

Library of Congress Number: 00-193365
ISBN #:   Softcover   0-7388-6004-2

All rights reserved. No part of this book may be reproduced or transmitted in any form or by any means, electronic or mechanical, including photocopying, recording, or by any information storage and retrieval system, without permission in writing from the copyright owner.

This is a work of fiction. Names, characters, places and incidents either are the product of the author's imagination or are used fictitiously, and any resemblance to any actual persons, living or dead, events, or locales is entirely coincidental.

This book was printed in the United States of America.

To order additional copies of this book, contact:
Xlibris Corporation
1-888-7-XLIBRIS
www.Xlibris.com
Orders@Xlibris.com

CONTENTS

Acknowledgements 9

PART I: THE WIND

Time Fill My Eyes 13
Hard Headed Woman 15
Songs From The Wood 21
Ruby Love 26
Love To Love You Baby 43
Bungle in the Jungle 53
Father and Son 58

PART II: SILENT SUNLIGHT

I Wish, I Wish 69
Trouble 77
Maybe You're Right 82
Wild World 90
If I Laugh 97
How Many Times 109

PART III: MOONSHADOW

Diamonds & Rust 117
Skating Away 128
Miles From Nowhere Tuesday's Dead 134
How Can I Tell You 137
Oh Very Young... 148
Morning Has Broken 154
EPILOGUE: Life's a Love Song 160

For you and for me,
thanks to Al.

Acknowledgements

With gratitude to readers: Gwen Moran, Barbara Kaden, Michelle Hill, Jamie Wells, Greg Loomis, Marvelene Beach, Andrea Miller, Nancy Wittenberg;
To legal eagle Janna Glasser for advice;
To Natalie Goldberg for the meaning of structure;
To Howard Treeger for reaching back to give a leg up to a neighborhood kid.

PART I: THE WIND

Time Fill My Eyes

Please, please, don't let me be late.

 I tugged hard at the heavy church door. It unexpectedly gave way, flying from my grasp. Inside was the hushed oppressive silence that weighs down the air just before a funeral. I headed for a rear pew but changed my mind. Instead, I slid unnoticed into one a few rows behind the family, his family. I was relieved to have a moment or two to collect myself. God, I can't believe I drove in the wrong direction for 20 minutes. Even my subconscious can't bear to be here. But here I sit, alone, a Jew in a Catholic Church, at the funeral of a man I hadn't heard so much as a whisper from in almost 15 years.

 The April evening was raw, but that's not why I couldn't stop shivering. Barely a week ago, Nick relayed the news that his brother Don was dead, pushing the words over the phone line breathlessly. He had been found the day before in an Oakland motel room, after his heart had given out—or perhaps given in—two months shy of his 40th birthday.

 In place of a casket was a wood box, not much larger than the type that holds cigars. *At least I don't have to confront some ghastly facsimile of him laid out in an open coffin.* Instead, two photos flanked the box. An angelic, sepia-tinted picture of a child at communion was vaguely familiar. But the other, a simple black and white close-up, sucked my breath away. It was the face of a young man caught in a moment of pure joy. It was the face I knew, the face I loved.

 When I could bring myself to look away, I noticed the yellow roses, my favorite. *They're everywhere. How eerie. So many times he had sent them to me.* I glanced down at the single yellow rose in my lap and shuddered. Lifting the bloom to my face I inhaled deeply, capturing its scent and blocking the lingering odor of incense, which always made my nose itch. The cloying aroma penetrated my nostrils anyway and lodged in my brain, evoking unbidden images of Don behind clouds of pot smoke.

My eyes roamed the tiny seaside church, searching for a familiar face. So few people. None of his childhood friends. I'm not sure why that surprised me. After all, he'd left the Jersey Shore for the West Coast years ago, refusing to return for so much as a quick visit. I never even liked most of his friends. Still, their absence reinforced my feeling of isolation.

Studying the backs of those in the front pews, I could make out his parents and sister, guessing that an unfamiliar back belonged to her husband. His mother's back was still and straight, stoically calm. Tears will come from the men in the family. I can find no one resembling Donald's ex-wife, Beth, or their daughter, Donna. Chagrined, I realized how much I wanted them here, how I longed to see Donna again. As an infant, she had been the picture of her mother. Now in her teens, I wondered how much of Don shone through those big brown eyes. After the divorce, Beth and I had greeted each other warmly at rare chance meetings, but that was years ago, before she remarried and moved to Atlanta. It's as if having shared a common love made us family, sort of distant cousins. Their absence made for more unfinished business.

My eyes settled on the broad back and dark ponytail directly in front of me. *Good God, that must be Nick. Let's see, by now he would be in his mid-thirties.* Gone was the lanky 17-year-old who arrived at my doorstep guitar in hand. I softly touched his shoulder. He turned his head, covering my hand with his own. For a second, I wasn't alone.

The music began. It was all too familiar, yet it caught me off-guard. The seductive voice of Cat Stevens drew me suffocatingly close, luring me back 20 years.

Hard Headed Woman

February 1975

 My feet ached and my arm was beginning to stiffen from the weight of the heavy glass door. Every time I leaned into it, my bra strap slid off my shoulder, cutting into the top of my arm. My blouse tugged at the waistband of my pants. Less than four hours into my shift and already I was downright cranky.
 Despite the bitter cold, the line waiting to get into the Back Bay Diner wrapped around the side of the building. With almost everyone having been ejected from a local bar at the 2 a.m. closing time, it wasn't a particularly merry bunch either. They were cold, hungry and not in the mood to be put on hold. But they had little choice, as the Back Bay was one of the few eateries at the Jersey Shore open all night.
 It was a normal Saturday night bar crowd for a mid-winter weekend. If it had been summer, the line would have snaked through the large parking lot swelled by Bennies, the locals' name for summer-folk. Still, it was 2:45 a.m. and the crowd showed no signs of slacking off. They called me a hostess, although the duties on my 11 p.m. to 7 a.m. shift had more in common with that of a bouncer at a bar. I was the first woman to hold the job, and hold it I did.
 The Back Bay was the nexus of the local Jersey Shore social scene, and with the drinking age at 18, the crowd was young and rowdy. The diner was a kind of a last chance saloon, with table-hopping in hopes of landing a bed partner as the rule. I often thought myself housemother to the world's longest-running frat party. The place did have a few standards, though. Those who

consistently dumped eggs on their waitress' head, were particularly vulgar or refused to wear shoes would find themselves exiled. Since being banned from the joint put a fatal crimp in their social lives, I wielded more clout than my 5-foot 3-inch frame would suggest. Of course, this didn't stop the line jumpers who were supposedly meeting people inside. By 3 a.m., playing the heavy got a bit old. I was glad I only had the role on weekends.

At 27, I had lived in Bay Harbor for seven years, having barely survived a brief marriage with one of its favorite sons. With Jeff gone, the kids and I lived in a converted summer bungalow within walking distance of the diner. I worked there on weekends, juggling college, kids and mountains of bills.

And so it was that night, business as usual. Then a young man in an olive green corduroy car coat, thick black hair falling across one brown eye, appeared at the door. As he pulled the glass door open, Susan, the formidable 6-foot tall red-haired cashier, drew her hand across her neck in an off-with-his-head motion, the signal that he was among the banned. I raised my arm to bar his entrance just as Susan realized she had mistaken him for one of his friends. He gazed down at me with disdain muttering "Yeah, right," as he brushed past, a cigarette dangling out of the corner of his mouth like a character in an old World War II movie.

Obnoxious little punk, I thought. But I was shaken. In the few seconds his face paused inches from mine something happened. The oversized jacket and the mop of thick hair gave off a waif-like look that belied his arrogance. I wanted to grab his hair and throttle him. I wanted to grab his hair. It didn't take me long to look forward to his coming in. He was always with his friends, of course, Frank, Marc or Warren. They would ask for the corner booth by the door, Don told me later, so he could watch me unobserved.

I did feel his eyes on me, however, the night Susan called the cops. It didn't happen often because the management frowned on the practice and put a great deal of pressure on waitresses not to sign complaints against patrons, regardless of how drunk or obnoxious. But that night I had come to the aid of a green young waitress being hammered by four drunks in the corner booth across from Don and his friends.

"What's the problem?" I asked the lead drunk.

"The fucking bitch messed up my order twice. I ordered over easy and these are hard as rocks." He waved the plate under my nose. "She refuses to take them back again."

I looked over at the waitress, who was shaking with anger and fighting back tears. I knew she hadn't messed up the order, that he was too far gone to remember what he had said. I also knew she was afraid to take it back into the kitchen for a second time. Our head cook was a burly man with a foul temper who was not above throwing rejected plates of eggs at waitresses on just such occasions.

"Let me see what I can do." As I reached for the plate, he made the mistake of grabbing my ass. That was enough for Susan.

Now, you don't work at an all-night diner anywhere without getting to know local constabulary, so the sergeant and patrolman who answered the call were friends, especially Sgt. Robert Ryan who worked steady nights. He strutted over to the table, tapping his nine-man-flashlight—so named because he claimed he could take out nine men with its long, weighted handle—against the open palm of his left hand.

"You wanna tell me what's going on," he directed the biggest offender with a stern face. It wasn't a question. "I understand you went beyond verbal abuse and got downright physical with this young lady." He pointed the flashlight at me and shot me a dead serious look.

I stood off to the side and listened while the jerk rattled on, lying his guts out. But when he insisted I was flirting with him and welcomed the manhandling, I blew up.

"Donkey dust!" I screamed in his face before stomping off.

After seeing the men to their cars, Ryan came back into the diner and pulled me aside, placing one very large hand on each of my shoulders.

"Donkey dust! Donkey dust," he exclaimed, waving his finger

at me. "Here I am, trying to maintain a professional demeanor and your contribution is donkey dust! It's a good thing you're one of my favorite people or . . ." He made a fist and mockingly punched me in the face. We burst out laughing.

"So sorry, Bobby," I gasped through my giggles. "I'll do my best from now on to keep my colorful language to myself in these situations."

As the name "Bobby" left my lips, I sensed Don's eyes narrow. Out of the corner of my eye, I could see him hunched over the table, drawing down hard on a cigarette. Nobody, but nobody, called Ryan "Bobby."

Don's way of getting my attention was akin to the ponytail pulling of a fourth grader. Being almost a decade his senior, I never dreamed the mischievous bad boy routine was for my benefit.

Like the time I wore a black knit pantsuit. The top was shaped like a very short dress, fitting snugly under the bust and flaring out over the hips. This being the 1970s, the slacks must have had at least a modest bell. Under the pants, I wore knee-high black, calf-hugging, high-heeled stretch boots so in vogue. Don was fascinated by the boots and kept bugging me about how they felt, how they fit, were they comfortable and so on. He goaded me into planting my leg up in the seat, hiking my pants to the knee and showing them to him. Months later, when we were living together, he watched me put them on, grinning. I looked up.

"I never could figure out what the deal was. Why were you so insistent on seeing these boots?"

He roared.

"I didn't give a damn about the boots, we—well, actually, I—wanted to get a look at your legs. And you laid your knee right under my nose. I was so hard, I had to sit there for 20 minutes after the guys left."

My jaw dropped open. I was the mother of two watching my 30th birthday barreling toward me. He was a year out of high school, working as a cook and still sleeping in his childhood bed.

He was cute, smart and very funny, but I hadn't thought much beyond that—or I didn't allow myself to.

One weeknight I was filling in for a waitress working the counter, when Don and Marc stumbled in. At 3 a.m., the diner was almost deserted. Surprised to see me, the two settled in at my counter. They were the only customers, so we chatted as they drank cups of coffee and munched on fries with gravy. We started to gossip about one of the older waitresses who always gave me a hard time. As she walked out of the kitchen, I leaned in close. By then I was looking for excuses to breathe his air.

"Now, don't look, but . . ." I hadn't so much as muttered the "but" when, in perfect unison, the pair turned smartly to look in the forbidden direction. I was simultaneously mortified and delighted.

Don would go on to describe in graphic detail later how he and the guys loved to sit at the counter if I was waitressing so they could watch me clean the huge coffee urns. They were so large we had to climb up on a stepladder to scrub the insides with a long handled brush. Evidently, the motion hiked up the back of my white uniform considerably more than modesty would allow.

Without realizing it, we started looking for ways to touch each other, going so far as to engage in an arm wrestling match at 4:30 a. m. one blustery morning during the lull between drunks and railroad men.

"I bet I could take ya," I bragged, making a show of sizing him up. As a young girl I had taken down guys twice my size. It was something about the way I was built, leverage seemed to be on my side. And I had learned how to use their own arrogance against them.

"You gotta be joking, woman," he shot back with a snort.

"Oh, yeah. Wanna feel my muscle?" I said, cocking my arm. He leaned over and gave the obligatory squeeze.

"Not bad . . . for a chick," he conceded with a shrug. "How much are you willing to put up?" He leaned back in the booth and took a hit off his ever-present Marlboro. "How about . . ." he blew several smoke rings, "you cook me dinner?"

"You're on. What do I get if I win?"

"I take you out for dinner, at a real restaurant, not here ... Deal?"

"Deal."

We squared off in the corner booth. At first I could tell he was toying with me, letting his arm fall off to the side. But when he had some trouble bringing it back upright, he realized I wasn't a pushover and he might really lose. The smile slid from his eyes and was replaced by concentration. I fought hard, I really did. He beat me, though, fair and square.

"So, when's dinner?"

"You really serious?"

"Deadly."

"You really want to come to dinner?"

"You can cook, can't you?"

"Of course I can cook," I snapped, hesitating for a beat. "I tell you what. Here's my number. You call me and we'll arrange a time."

Although I thought he was merely showboating for his friends, I took a napkin from the holder, borrowed a pen from Susan and scribbled my number down. I can see his face to this day, as he reached over the table to take the paper from my hand. He was grinning.

Songs From The Wood

I could never remember what I served for dinner that night, the night Don finally made it to my house. It had taken him several weeks after I gave him my phone number to work up the guts to call. I had just about given up thinking it would ever happen, when, as it so often does, the phone rang. I recognized the deep, sweet tones of his voice immediately.

"Are we still on for dinner?"

"Sure," I replied. "I'm no welcher."

We spoke for almost two hours, a portent of things to come. He told me that he'd always known he was going to be a writer, about his journals, his practice of writing every day for 30 minutes. He told me how bored he was of menial-job-days and barhopping nights, and how much he looked forward to getting on to college.

"I'm sick and tired of playing coy little virgin games with post-adolescent girls with peas for brains," he said. "And there's this loony ex-girlfriend of mine that won't leave me alone. She follows me around, driving me and my whole family crazy."

"Were you her first real love?"

"Yeah. And if she doesn't cut this shit out soon, I may just be her last."

When he spoke of her obsessive phone calls numbering into the hundreds each week, his voice took on the naked desperate quality of someone who needed out. The Seaside Park house he lived in with his parents and kid brother and sister was starting to close in on him, he added.

I told him that almost as soon as I could talk, I announced to anyone within earshot that I was going to be an actress. I told him

I would practice singing and dancing in front of the only mirror in my house big enough, even though it meant standing on the coffee table in the living room of our Long Island home.

"So what stopped you?"

"I did a first class job of derailing myself when I married Jeff. The marriage may be over, but the debts remain. My husband was long on charm and short on responsibility. Even when we were together, the paychecks had been sporadic. Now, forget it."

Before locking the door behind him, though, I had insisted he sign the house—and two mortgages—over to me.

"Now, all I have to do is find a way to support the four of us... me, Lizzie, Josh and the house," I said. "We barely get by on my educational loans and grants. That's where the diner comes in."

"I wondered what a nice Jewish girl like you was doing in Bay Harbor. How come you stay?"

"It's easier in a small town," I explained. "I don't think I could handle living in a city. In the suburbs, kids need a full-time parent, someone to drive them everywhere. Here, Lizzie and Josh can get by on a bike, and I can count on the local cops to keep an eye on them when I'm not around."

"So I noticed."

"Noticed, what?"

"How you can count on the local cops."

"So you did."

"What's the deal with you and that pig Ryan, anyway?"

"I'm afraid I don't understand the question, counselor," I replied with all the sarcasm I could muster. "Would you care to rephrase?"

"Not really... Oh... just forget it."

"Wise choice."

Easing off of that subject, I told him I was lonely and often scared. I was wearing out, I said, and feared I would run out of steam before earning my degree, doomed to eternal duty monitoring the door at the Back Bay, gatekeeper to my own private hell.

He almost didn't make it to my house for dinner. The night before, some drunk lost control of his car while careening down the street in front of Don's home, totaling his well-seasoned Chevy. When he called, I couldn't hide the disappointment in my voice. But Don did something then only a 19-year-old male, in the grip of his hormones, would do. In the middle of winter, he hitchhiked the 10 miles to my house, clutching a bottle of Mateus.

Down the road, he would jokingly accuse me of throwing him to the wolves. When he arrived, I ushered him upstairs to the playroom with the kids while I finished setting the table. In reality, I thought I was doing him a favor, as I was almost always more comfortable with little children in a strange place.

We ate at the old oak pedestal table in the kitchen, the children taking turns showing off to catch the attention of our guest. It was predictably hard to get them into bed that evening. Once they settled down, we turned our full attention on each other for the first time.

For someone who entered this world on the summer solstice, Donald James DeLuca's hair, eyes, complexion and temperament were all intensely dark and brooding. Beneath it, though, flowed a river of good humor and intelligence. A bit more compact than average in height and build, his hands and feet were singularly delicate and well shaped, his movements fluid. His brown eyes had remarkable depth and sensuality, proficient at encircling their object—in this case me—like a silky fur cape.

I curled up on the far end of the tan corduroy sofa, the wale worn flat in many spots. Without hesitation, he sat beside me, taking my hand in his, lightly stroking the length of my palm with his finger. That's all. He didn't move to kiss me or take me in his arms but continued slowing caressing the inside of my hand. I kept thinking I would pull my hand away but couldn't bring myself to move. Gradually, my concentration came to a point at the center of my palm. When he lifted a finger to his mouth, the spell was momentarily broken and I pulled my hand back. He smiled and gently shook his head, as if I was a child trying to hide candy.

Taking my hand once again he lifted it to his lips and continued caressing my palm with his tongue, outlining every crease, every fold, every finger. I started to shake. I couldn't say exactly when or even how our clothes came off. Nor could I pinpoint the moment he entered me.

When my senses cleared a bit, I turned my head and found him looking over at me, his head resting in a cupped palm. He was grinning. Much to my dismay, I found myself grinning back. Our eyes locked and we started to laugh. My whole body was tingling, as if tiny droplets of cool water danced across my skin. When I finally took in the scene, we were both naked on the red shag rug in front of the couch. I'm still not sure how we got there.

Oh, shit, I thought, *I must be out of my mind.*

But before I could get up, I felt the soft pressure of his lips at my ankle, slowly working up the inside of my leg, provoking a sharp involuntary intake of breath, something between a sigh and a moan. His lips and tongue reached the top of my thighs and played for what seemed like an eternity, teasing and probing very lightly. I stifled a scream. He rolled over and pulled me on top of him, grabbing my rear and thrusting deep inside me, controlling the depth and speed of the strokes with his hands, irregular at first, deliberately non-rhythmic. Then he held me up, pushing the weight of my body off his a bit, teasing, and when he brought me back down hard something inside me gave way. I couldn't have stopped it if I wanted to. I exploded in great waves, one after another. And a few moments later so did he.

"You are incredibly beautiful when you climax," he said. We were dripping with sweat and still clinging to one another. If I wasn't in love with him before, I was then.

"I'll have to take your word for it," I gasped. "No one has ever seen me before. You're the first."

He looked at me in disbelief for a few seconds. Then he cupped my face in his hands, like my dad used to do when I was a little girl. No doubt, I felt like the younger of the two. His eyes searched my face and he tenderly kissed my forehead. We dropped off to sleep right there, my head on his shoulder. I awoke several hours later to his outstretched hand, leading me upstairs to my bedroom. We made love one more time before he left.

He moved in shortly after that. For some months, sex was our major form of recreation, my own private Summer of Love. He had never had it on tap, so to speak, never awakened to find a willing loving partner, someone he didn't have to work at seducing. I was delirious. He was young, beautiful, and I, too, had never had a partner such as him, someone so interested and delighted in my body and mind. When we weren't making love, we were making coffee, eating and talking, talking, talking. *What could be better,* I thought, *than a man who is great in bed, finds your body and mind fascinating, and loves to eat?*

My poor kids ate a lot of cold cereal that summer waiting for us to come out from behind a locked bedroom door. When they were at their father's or my folks, we would often lock the doors and shut off the phone, content to simply be in each other's company. It drove everyone else to distraction, but we didn't care.

"Where the hell have you been," his friend Frank barked at me one Sunday night when I answered the banging at the door. "I've been calling for days."

"Whatever do you mean?" I smiled. "We've been home all weekend. Isn't that so, Don?" I called into the kitchen.

Don appeared and walked over to the door, grinning.

"Gee, honey, did we forget we shut those darn phones off, again? Sorry Frank," Don said in an unconvincing tone. "We were kinda occupied. What's up?"

"What the hell difference does it make now," Frank sneered, looking my way.

My folks were none too thrilled, either. They were still in shock over my new living arrangement, and I really would sometimes forget to turn the phone back on for days, which whipped them into a frenzy of concern. After a while, I would paste a "phone off" note to the kitchen extension to remind me.

Ruby Love

8 June 1975
Dearest Deborah,
I don't believe that ever in my life have I been at quite this loss for words. No term paper or final exam or "Dear Jane" letter has ever posed such a terribly difficult problem as this note on the inside of a birthday card, for Christ sakes. Perhaps partly it's because I love and need you as I do. Mostly, I think, it's because no matter what I write or say or do for the rest of my life—it's not enough to repay you for all the happiness you've given me in two months.

You joked once about "broadening my horizons" and the funniest part of it was that it wasn't funny. I have never felt so very content with simply being alive, being with you, being around you. I realize this is terribly trite, but if I were to wake up tomorrow and find this has all been a dream, it would be worth the time and effort and disappointment of reaching to my left and finding just a pillow. You've changed me; you've changed my life; you've made me five times the person I was simply by loving me - really loving me. You've made me as happy as anyone could ever hope to be.

All my love,
Don
P. S. I think that I'm probably the only person I know with a birthday in two different years . . . Love, me.

It was a toss-up as to who was more upset about Don moving in with the kids and me.

My folks were predictably shocked but reversed their usual

roles. My normally placid mother recoiled in horror: "Oh, my God, you don't mean that BOY!" My usually belligerent father, on the other hand, retreated into hurt silence, refusing to acknowledge Don's presence whenever possible. This was tougher to take, since I'd always thought of myself as being closer to my dad. It was as if I had insulted him personally with my choice. I never could wrap my mind around why that was. Not only did they share the same dark, good looks and body type, but both had beautifully shaped hands and small feet, almost dainty in a man. My grandmother, though, adored him. And when she referred to him as "that boy" we both smiled.

My parents had been slipping me some money every month, so they tried to use that as leverage, hinting strongly that they were not disposed to help support the young man in question. It didn't work. Any added expense brought on by Don's moving in, I insisted, would be more than off-set by the money I would save in child care, as he agreed to watch the kids while I was in class.

Don handled his parents in true adolescent style—he didn't tell them, not the whole story, anyway. He simply announced he was moving in with "a girl named Debbie." His practical, down-to-earth mom put on a stern but reasonable face and tried to talk him out of it. Just about what I would have done in her place. His father was outright furious. His younger siblings thought it was cool and fought over who would inherit his room. A month or so later he fessed up to the truth, and his relationship with his family became even more labored.

My best friend Carin accused me of caving in to lust at the expense of my children.

"How can you expose your children to this?"

"Expose them to what, the fact that I'm a human being, that I have a life beyond being a mother?"

"You know what I mean."

"Yeah, I do," I shot back, "and I don't like it one bit."

The one I had the most trouble telling was Bobby Ryan, so I kept putting it off. Everyone in town assumed that Bobby and I were having an affair, that I had become a member of his constantly changing harem. Bobby never let his marriage vows stand in the way of a good time, and the hours he worked as a cop left him free to roam while most men were at work. His dark blond curly locks and navy blue eyes gave him an eternally boyish quality many women, me included, have a hard time passing by.

But it wasn't that simple between us. What had started out as another fling had taken a strange and unsettling turn—more than friends and less than lovers. The later was his choice and a constant frustration for me. He made a show of crude sexual teasing in public, but that was it. If Howard Stern had been a cop, he would have been Bobby Ryan.

"Are you smuggling grapefruits out of the diner?" he would say loudly, glancing down at my generous breasts. If I dared wear a tube top, he would often tug at the top and peer down. His behavior infuriated Carin.

"How can you let him do that stuff? I don't understand. It's just not like you."

"I know. But I can't seem to work up a good mad at the guy."

Mostly, he would wake me up at 2 a.m. with a phone call. "Coffee on?" It was more of a demand than a question.

"OK," I'd reply in a sleep-filled voice.

He'd wander over, and we would sit and talk. More often than not, he had just crawled out of bed with one chickie or another. The conversation would be all over the map, depending on how much he had to drink.

"Deborah," he said solemnly one night. I looked up. "Promise me something . . ."

"What?"

"Promise me you'll never let a guy handcuff you."

I started to laugh, but he wasn't smiling.

"I'm not kidding. No matter what a guy says, no matter how much you trust him . . . don't do it. Once you're handcuffed you're totally helpless."

"Well, it hasn't come up," I answered, suppressing a smile. "But if it does, I promise to keep your advice in mind. It's nice to know you care."

He was silent for a minute or two, seemingly deep in thought.

"You know, you're the smartest woman I've ever met."

"How much have you had to drink?"

"I'm not shit-faced. I mean it. I know I take advantage of you. I want you to know I'm sorry for that. But I know I'll do it again."

"So what else is new?"

"The truth is, you scare the living shit outta me," he conceded.

"That's why you won't sleep with me, right?"

"Right, Miss Smartee Pants."

"You guys are all alike, pulled in by the tits and scared witless when you realize the boobs came with a brain attached."

Don had already moved in by the time I was forced into spilling the beans to Bobby. He stopped by the house on some pretext or another late one afternoon, a rare occurrence.

"Hey, what's happening?" Bobby asked when I opened the door.

Startled to see him, I stuttered "Nothin' much, why?"

"Aren't you gonna invite me in?" he grinned.

Reluctantly, I opened the door. I suspected he had heard rumors and came to check things out. Don was in the kitchen with the kids when we walked in. I made the absolutely unnecessary introductions and the two sat down next to one another at the counter, Bobby's burly body dwarfing Don's.

"Why don't you guys watch Sesame Street upstairs in my bedroom," I told the kids. Delighted by being allowed into my jealously guarded private space, they scampered off. "Lizzie, you can turn the set on, right?" I called after them. I wasn't about to leave the two guys alone, even for a moment.

I was scared stiff. *This is stupid,* I thought. *What can happen? He's not going to take out his gun and shoot everyone. Just tell him. Spit it out.* I couldn't stand still and became very busy cleaning up the kitchen and preparing dinner, clanking pots. I glanced over at the counter and detected a look in Don's eyes I couldn't define. Both of their mouths were turned up in an imitation of a smile. I dropped a pot on my foot. *Enough!*

"Guess what, Bobby?" I said, my voice tight and high, in a vain attempt to be casual, "Don's going to be staying here for a while."

"That so?" Bobby replied, raising an eyebrow. He took a shade longer than necessary to light a cigarette. "Got any coffee on?"

Involuntarily, my eyes shot over to Don. He had leaned back slightly on the stool, his arms folded across his chest loosely. That's when the look registered. It was the self-satisfied look of the cat that had swallowed the canary.

The rest of the conversation was a blur. But after one cup of coffee, Bobby got up to leave, shooting me a walk-me-out-to-the-car look. We had hardly cleared the porch when he exploded.

"What the hell is wrong with you! Are you nuts . . . living with that little piss ant kid?"

"Why does everyone keep saying that?" I yelled back. Suddenly, I was more angry then scared, tired of all the criticism. "What's the matter, is this gonna inconvenience you? Well, you know what? You'll have to get over it. So will my parents, his parents, Carin and the whole fucking town for all I care!"

"Take it easy," Bobby said lightly, taken aback by me response. "You're getting shrill . . . Do me a favor, be careful . . ."

"Yeah, yeah," I cut in, "I won't let him handcuff me. I promise." It had become a running joke.

" I'm afraid he already has," he said quietly, as I turned to walk into the house.

Frank, too, was put out big time, resenting all the time and energy Don directed my way, although nothing was ever said out loud. Our exchanges were almost always exceedingly polite, too polite.

Frank Talerico was Don's best friend and my worst enemy. Physically they were opposites, as far as the bar scene went, a complementary pair. Frank was an ice blond with angelic coloring that ran contrary to his true nature. He sported a goatee, which further accentuated his pointy features, and his fine hair curled onto his shoulders. Roughly 6-foot-tall and thin to the point of boniness, there was nothing about him that would invite closeness. His blue eyes were a watery shade, like that of a shallow puddle, pale to the point of translucence. He contentedly worked in his dad's auto body shop and had as much ambition as intellectual depth.

When I was within earshot, he hid behind an Eddie Haskel-like show of respect. I went along with the charade but was not taken in. I knew that as soon as the two were out the door, the snide, dirty, older woman jokes surfaced. The tension between us did not escape Don's notice, but best friend or no, he was intent on hanging on to this thing we had. It was a bit like trying to land a huge marlin in choppy seas, he once said, unpredictable, even a might painful at times, but a helluva lot of fun.

For us it was simple, or so we thought. We were crazy about each other, the sex was great and it would be practical for us to be together, to live together. He would bring me companionship and a measure of help with the children. He would enrich my world; I would expand his. He would have the freedom of living away from his parents, yet still have a family to come home to. Both of us were to continue seeing other people. It was all so rational it would have done Mr. Spock proud. Unfortunately, neither of us were Vulcans. Sure enough, before my 28th birthday the landscape had changed considerably.

One Thursday morning in May, I was getting ready to leave for class when Don stumbled down the stairs, half-asleep. Wednesday night was a big bar night and he usually woke up hard the next morning. He had a strange look on his face and turned away when I went to kiss him good-by.

"What's wrong?"

"Nothing," he shrugged. "It's just that I woke up with this rash on my face that's driving me nuts."

Over his protestations, I tilted his face toward the window to get a better look. Sure enough, the skin around his mouth and nose was raw.

"Lemme put something on that," I said, reaching for a tube of hydrocortisone cream stored on top of the refrigerator. He tried to sit obediently still while I ever so gently smoothed on the salve, but the area was so tender he squirmed at the slightest pressure. I touched a particularly sore red spot and he jumped. "Ouch."

"That really hurts, huh, babe? I'm sorry. Just hang on for another minute and I'll be done... What the hell could have done this to you?"

He looked so miserable. My mind flailed around for an outrageous joke, anything to distract him, to make him feel better.

"I don't know, pal. It sure looks like a bad case of 'cunt burn' to me," I blurted. As soon as the words brushed past my lips I regretted it. Instead of coming back at me with the expected smart remark, his face turned ashen.

Oh shit, what am I going to do now? I prattled on mindlessly about the supposed ailment I'd invented, trying to regain my composure. It was too late. Pain swelled up inside as I grabbed my books and ran from the house blinking back tears. I could barely bring myself to look at him that night. Reasonable or not, I felt betrayed. Until then, his bar hopping with Frank hadn't bothered me. I assumed he danced and flirted like hell, but hadn't allowed myself to consider anything more intimate. Now, I could no longer pretend.

Don was beside himself. He couldn't figure out what was going on. Through the windows he could see bulbs sprouting, but inside those windows frost might have well been forming, such was the temperature between us. He could tell I'd been crying but didn't seem to know how to approach me. I just kept cleaning things, the same things over and over. I could see he was frightened but didn't care.

A full day passed in this polite coldness. Late Friday afternoon, the kids left to spend the weekend with Jeff. Once they were out of the house, I excused myself to take a nap before work, making it clear I wasn't in the mood for company.

Crossing the parking lot on the way into the diner, a patrol car criss-crossed in my path, driving in circles to get my attention. I knew it was Bobby and ignored it. It stopped dead in my path and I was hit full force by the car's searchlight.

"Whoa there, young lady," a voice bellowed over the loudspeaker.

I kept walking. This was not part of the game. Bobby got out of the car as I passed and grabbed me.

"Wait... What's going on? Are you all right? Is anything the matter with the kids?"

"The kids are fine... and I don't want to talk about it. OK?"

"No, it's not OK."

"Please Bobby, I can't." I tied to yank myself free, and when he saw the tears in my eyes he loosened his grip and let me go.

"It's that piss ant you've taken up with, isn't it?" he spit. I turned and walked inside without answering. Bobby came in late for his coffee break that night. It was almost 3 a.m. and the diner was fairly quiet. I tried to stay busy sorting through menus, but he wasn't having it.

"Sit down with me for a minute."

"I can't; I'm working."

"The hell you are. Sue, it's OK if Deb takes a break isn't it?... See, it's just fine with her. Sit," he ordered in his shift commander's voice. I sat.

"Now tell me what the hell happened."

"No."

"I promise I won't say 'I told you so.'"

I snorted. "Yeah, right." Just then Don and Frank walked in, obviously coming off a long night of partying. Without thinking, I started to get up, but Bobby quickly leaned toward me, as if to murmur a confidence, placing his right hand on my left shoulder in what looked like a light friendly gesture. It may have been friendly, but it was anything but light. He quietly applied just enough pressure to preventing me from standing. Don and Frank glared at me before turning toward the counter. I was shaking.

"What are you doing?" I demanded. Bobby leaned closer and whispered in my ear. "Let the little shit squirm. Look at me and smile. Good girl." He reached around and tickled me a bit on the side. I laughed. "That's better." We sat together for some time with him animatedly relating one story after another, pausing from time to time to whisper in my ear.

"I'm OK Bobby, really. I have to get up."

"Do you promise not to go running over there?"

"Yes, I promise. I'll just go back to working on the breakfast menus."

True to my word, I stayed behind the cash register and turned my full attention on the menus. In her usual protective mode, Susan placed her substantial body between me and the rest of the diner, affording me a measure of privacy. Shortly after Bobby went back out on the road, Don and Frank swallowed the last of their coffee and left. We didn't speak.

It was almost 7:30 by the time I left the Back Bay that morning. I wasn't in any hurry to get home to Don. As I made my way slowly across the parking lot, I caught sight of a reflection in the dew-laden macadam. Looking up, I was stunned to see Bobby dressed in civvies, leaning against his silver Corvette, smoking.

"Get in." He held the door open for me.

"What has gotten into you?" I protested. "I have to get home."

"I thought the kids were with Jeff," he said.

"They are."

"So what's the rush?" He continued to hold the door. I opened my mouth to object once more but he cut me off. "Could you, for once, just be quiet and do as you're told? Put your sweet ass in the seat." I slid into the car with a sigh.

"Where are we going?" He didn't answer. I leaned back in deep bucket seat, inhaled the leather scent and closed my eyes. When I felt the car stop, I sat up. We were at the Point Beach jetty, one of my favorite places. I smiled.

The jetty was at the north end of the mile-long Point Pleasant Beach boardwalk, far from the sound of amusement rides and the smell of sausage and fries. Across the inlet, on the Manasquan side, a matching finger of rock protruded into the Atlantic Ocean. It marked the beginning of the inland waterway and I often rode my bike there from the diner to watch the early morning fishing boats venture forth. On my rare forays to the beach, I always lay my towel on the Point side, close to the jetty. I loved the sound of the water as it swirled around and through the intricate pattern of rocks and could lose myself for hours staring down at the eddies.

"Come on," he tugged at me. I slipped off my shoes as he reached behind his seat and picked up a plaid blanket and a thermos. I recoiled in mock horror.

"Oh no . . . not the Bobby Blanket!" I had often teased him about his habit of carrying it "just in case." As any shore dweller knows, sand and sex only mesh in the movies. I scrunched up my face. "Yuck . . . When did you wash that thing last?"

"Very funny," he snapped, pulling me out of the car.

We climbed out onto the jetty and walked to the end on the flat surface, sitting down facing a calm ocean. The only sounds came from the waves, the gulls and the occasional plop of a fishing line hitting the water or being reeled in. I leaned back on my elbows and breathed deeply, enjoying the sight of Bobby's back outlined in the morning sun against the blue sky and sea.

"Here," he handed me a cup of what looked like tomato juice. He poured himself a cup and put the thermos down.

Instead of taking a sip, I sniffed at the drink, dipped in a finger and licked it off. Bobby laughed. "I knew you'd do that." It was a not-so-bloody Mary, mostly vodka.

"Oh yeah, this is JUST what I need." I put the cup down. "You know I can't drink."

Bobby picked it up and handed it back. "It is what you need. It wouldn't hurt you to get a little snookered and let down a bit." I hesitated. "It's OK, Deb. I'll take care of you. I promise . . . Come 'ere." He spread his legs, patting the stone. I slid between them and let my back fall against his chest. The sun was warm on my face and Bobby warmed my back. His body enveloped me and I felt like a little girl, sheltered and safe. We drank in silence for some time before he spoke softly into my ear.

"It's time, Deb. Fill me in on why I should break one of his more significant bones."

"How about his jaw? It would be most satisfying to see it wired shut." I related the whole story.

"Cunt burn?" he roared with laughter. "Where the hell did that come from? I don't think I've ever heard you use that word."

"Haven't the foggiest. My psych prof would probably say I unconsciously recognized the rash for what it was and named it appropriate to my true feelings."

"What are you gonna do?" he asked gently.

"I don't know. I mean, according to our arrangement, he had every right to do as he pleased, but that doesn't make it hurt any less." I took a large swallow from the cup. It went down hard.

"Bobby?"

"What?"

"Am I really the smartest woman you ever met?"

"Far and away, my sweet."

"Then why didn't I see this coming?"

"Cause the operative word here is 'woman,' not 'smart.' " He paused and lit a cigarette. "You're in love with him, aren't you?"

" 'fraid so."

"Your choice in men confounds me."

"Present company excepted, I assume."

"You assume wrong," he replied, knocking gently on my head with an enormous fist. "Why the hell did you ever marry Jeff? He was even a turd in high school."

"I was 20 years old, desperate to get out from under my parents and without the guts to leave on my own, I guess. So I convinced myself I was in love with him. I just wanted to live together, though. Getting married was his idea, although I did try to make it work."

"What really happened between you two?"

"You mean, besides my realizing I didn't love him? . . . Lizzie, for one. Josh, for another . . . that makes twice . . . I wasn't much of a 'wife' and he took it out on me by cutting me off. One night, after he'd gone to bed at 9 for the fifth night in a row, something snapped. I left him with the kids and went out . . . and the rest is Back Bay history . . ."

I tilted my head back and looked into those bottomless blue eyes for a long minute, stroking his cheek with the fingertips of my right hand. The stubble of his beard was rough beneath my fingers. It felt good. He took my hand in his, lightly brushing his lips across tips of my fingers. I let my hand fall to my side.

"Bobby . . ."

"Don't."

"Please."

"No . . . absolutely not . . . You're not using me to get back at that pecker head."

"I thought you were all for 'revenge fucks'."

"Only if I'm the fucker, not the fucked . . . and not with you, kiddo." He glanced down at his watch. "Time to go."

"What? You have a date?" I sneered.

"As a matter of fact, I do." He pulled me to feet. I brushed the blown sand from my sage green trousers.

"Do you have any idea how much I hate you right now?"

"I doubt it," he answered, wrapping his arm around my shoulder.

The short ride to my house was silent. I jumped out before the car had fully come to a halt. Bobby called me back.

"Hey . . . I forgot. One more thing." He motioned for me to lean in close and kissed me full and deeply on the mouth. "That's for the jerk peering at us from your bedroom window . . . and this is for me," he added, cradling my face and kissing my eyes.

"Do you have any idea how much I love you now?" I croaked, eyes watering.

"I doubt it," he grinned, putting the vette into gear and peeling off.

I stood in the living room, listening as Don heavily and slowly descended the stairs. We stood facing each other on the spot where we had first made love. He braced himself, managing to look both hurt and angry at the same time.

"That was some little act you played out there with Ryan," he began. I didn't respond. "Well, aren't you going to say anything?" he jabbed at me with his voice. Then he noticed the glazed look in my eyes.

"You were out drinking . . . with HIM? I'm sitting here, wondering where the hell you are, worrying, and you're out tilting a few with that pig!"

I managed a short laugh. "It doesn't feel very good, does it?"

He was silent for a minute. Then walked over and put his hands on my shoulders. "You've made your point. Please, Deborah . . . don't do this, especially with Ryan."

I started to come back with "Do what?" but thought better of it. It took a few moments for me to gather the strength to open my mouth. I felt weary and dull, as if I hadn't slept in days. As I started to speak, he drew in a quick, sharp breath and held it.

"I can't handle this," I snapped, surprised by the strength in my voice. "This isn't working. I'm not cut out to be anybody's home base. It isn't enough. I thought it would be, but it's not. I need more from a relationship."

Don started to cry.

"God, I don't want to lose you. I've been sitting here trying to imagine my days—not to mention my nights—without your scent or weird laugh, without your body or that maze you call a mind. How could this have happened so fast? Damn it. How could this have happened at all? It wasn't supposed to be like this."

His shoulders shook with sobs, and my own hurt and anger began to wash away. *Holy shit, he really does care for me.* Don collapsed on the sofa. After a few minutes, I sat opposite him on the cedar chest, our knees touching. Cupping his face in my hands, I lightly wiped away the tears. When he noticed I was crying also, he did the same. We started laughing and fell into each other's arms onto the couch.

"Please," he whispered into my ear, "please, can we work this out? I'm so sorry. I had no idea it would hurt you like this. I had no idea it would hurt me like this."

"I should have known better than to believe an arrangement like this could work," I said, shaking him off and turning away. "I can't go through this again, I won't."

"What are we going to do?" he asked.

"I'm not sure. I don't want to see anyone else, and I don't want you to either. Are you willing to do that?"

"I don't know," he shook his head from side to side. "I can't bear the thought of losing what we have. I don't want to leave, but for Christ sake Deb, I'm only 19."

"Well, I suppose you could start by being more particular where you put your sweet mouth," I suggested with a forced grin.

"I think I may be losing my touch, anyway," he added with a slight smile. "The other night, some sweet young thing said I reminded her of a summer's eve."

"What's so bad about that?"

"I didn't get it at first either," he said wryly. "Then I realized she was calling me a douche."

We never actually resolved the monogamy issue, not in so many words. Rather, it faded away. We became too busy sniffing out and around each other's landscape.

"What time is it?" he'd ask.

"9:15," I'd answer.

"Aren't you gonna look at your watch?"

"I'm not wearing one."

"Well, how the hell do you know what time it is?"

"I don't know. I just do."

At first, he would go out of his way to check the time. Then, he would turn to me suddenly and ask, as if trying to sneak up on me. But after a few weeks, he just accepted me as his own personal living timepiece, something else his friends didn't have. I confess to getting a huge kick out his first-kid-on-the-block-with-a-new-toy attitude.

Don took pride and delight at my knowledge of baseball and football. Initially, he tested me with arcane rules questions, such as baseball's infield fly rule. After a time, when he found he couldn't trip me up, he would urge his friends to ask me this or that or place bets on me, like a parent showing off a precocious offspring. His friends, of course, had no way of knowing I had been a fanatical Yankee and Giants fan, even as a young girl living in Brooklyn. My teen-aged sexual fantasies revolved around Mickey Mantle and Y.A. Tittle as other girls' did around Fabian and Elvis.

He also got a real charge out of me being proofed at the door of a bar. Don would breeze past the bouncer and stand inside with a shit eating grin, as I dug out my wallet to prove I was 18 years old. He basked in the illusion of being older than I, albeit momentarily.

Then there were all those first year mundane domestic adjustments.

I would pull the shower curtain closed after I got out so the curtain could dry, like my mom taught me. He insisted it stay open so the tub could dry, like his mom taught him. I never could convince him to start with cold water when making coffee.

"If you're going to boil it anyway, what's the difference, might as well get a head start," he'd insist.

He never could convince me to iron a shirt the way his mom did. Then again, he never could convince me to iron, period.

Our first long car trip together was a pleasant eye opener. The foray to Connecticut for my cousin's wedding was an unexpected delight. We all had such a good time. There was no pressure, no rush, with Don eagerly pausing along the way to stretch and let the kids out or just checkout a weird looking bush.

"Did you ever wonder why we say thank-you to people in toll booths when we're giving *them* the money," he remarked.

How different from Jeff, to whom a car trip was merely an opportunity to best his last time, who barely slowed down at toll booths and would stop only grudgingly for bladder emergencies.

The tension; the fighting. I always arrived at our destination rigid with fatigue.

The wedding itself was even enjoyable. Usually, I sat on the sidelines all night waiting for my father to take a break from squiring my mom around the dance floor. Then I would get my turn at a dance or two. Once my dad had enough to drink, we might chance to jitterbug. Jeff had been as useless on the dance floor as he was in bed, but Don loved to dance as much as I did. And he could really move. I finally had a real dance partner, one who helped me add both the Hustle and the Bump to my ballroom dance repertoire.

The next weekend the kids were with Jeff, we took a trip alone, a day excursion to New Hope, Pennsylvania. We spent a bright spring Sunday lolling around the artsy town taking in the sights. In a cluttered Indian jewelry shop, Don bought me a pair of flashy but inexpensive filigree brass earrings, which dusted my shoulders as I walked. At a used-book store, he picked up a science fiction paperback and perused the back cover, tossing it aside with obvious disdain.

"Invisibility. What hogwash," he muttered under his breath.

"I thought you liked science fiction."

"Invisibility isn't science fiction, it's just plain fiction. I hate it when they write about stuff that just can't be," he added, launching into a detailed explanation of the properties of light waves that made invisibility impossible. It was my first exposure to the depth of his science fiction passion. And while I appreciated it, I was disappointed. I liked the idea of invisibility.

Having little money, we had packed some sandwiches and headed back to car for a late lunch just as the sky opened. We huddled in the car, eating, talking and laughing until the storm passed before heading home. That's when we saw the rainbow off in the distance. We looked at each other for a quiet minute before bursting into laughter.

"Well, what do ya say?" he asked, in mock seriousness.

"Why not," I laughed. "I wouldn't mind a small pot of gold. It'll look smashing on the coffee table."

So he slipped the car into gear and off we and dashed off in a vain search for the end.

On the ride home he fell quiet.

"What's wrong, babe?" I asked.

"Oh, nothin."

"Something is bothering you," I insisted. "You're actually pouting. Just spit it out."

"Back at the book store, you called some guy by my name."

"Your name? I called someone Don?"

"Duh . . . No, you called him babe."

I didn't worry so much about other women after that.

Love To Love You Baby

Right off, it was one of those *frisson* things. What was it called in *The Godfather*? Oh, yeah, *the lightning bolt*. Even that first night in the diner, the air between us was so charged I was surprised silverware didn't fly at us from around the room.

After that first explosion on the living room rug, it was a few weeks before we made love again. I think when we sobered up, terror set in—at least it did for me. I was, after all, a woman who had carried and given birth to a pair of substantial infants, and my body wore the evidence. It's not that I was hard on the eyes or anything, to a grown man. But Don was so young, and no way did I have the smooth body of a 16-year-old. Blessedly, the eyes of love are as generous as they are wide.

"Deb . . ." Don said in a tentative voice early one morning.

"Yes," I replied, rolling over and smiling into those eyes. We had lived together for about two weeks and each time we made love was better than the time before. He was infinitely slow and tender.

"Did you really climax for the first time that night on the living room rug?"

"Yes . . . why do you ask?"

"It's just so hard to understand. Didn't you enjoy sex with your husband? I mean, was he your first?"

I laughed. "No, he was far from my first and thank God even farther from my last! . . . You really want to know?"

"Yeah, I do," he said, sitting up and lighting a cigarette.

"OK . . . As you can imagine, I've given the subject a great deal of thought over the years. How far back do you want me to go?"

"All the way," he grinned. "I really like it when we go all the way." He bent down and nipped at my breast." I shook him off.

"Down boy . . . or I can't concentrate."

"Well, when I was a kid, back in the wild and woolly ancient 1960s, the birth control pill was the big thing. We could finally have sex without worrying about getting knocked up."

"So guys started expecting it," he cut in.

"Yeah . . . What made you say that?"

" 'Cause it's pretty much the same, now."

"I felt as though I had to have a reason to say 'no' instead of the other way around," I continued. "And I had a lot of sex that amounted to little more than a mechanical in-and-out."

"What about your girl friends?"

"We talked about sex all the time, of course, but I'm sure none of us had a clue of what an orgasm with a guy was all about . . . It wasn't until after I gave birth to Lizzie that I had friends who even mentioned the word masturbate."

"You know, with all this liberation hullabaloo, I don't think things have changed all that much for girls even now," he ventured.

"By the time Jeff put in an appearance, I was relentless in my search for the sacred orgasm I was sure every women in the world had but me . . . Unfortunately, Jeff lost interest in sex as soon as we married. Nothing provoked a response, even going to bed stark naked in the hope we might bump into each other and ignite something. There are some disadvantages to king-sized beds, that's for sure."

"I don't get it. How could he lie here night after night and not even touch you?"

"He seemed to manage it quite easily, actually. I could never make up my mind if he was inept because he was uninterested or uninterested because he was inept. Either way, the results were the same . . . until you came along, my sweet young thing." I kissed him quickly on the chest.

Don stubbed out his cigarette and lunged on top of me, burying his head between my legs. I let out a shriek of surprised delight.

"Shhh . . . you'll wake the kids."

I was nuts about his body, almost obsessed. His skin was velvety and the hair on his chest fine and silky like the hair on his head. Oh, that mop, strands of black hair, hinting at brown that framed his brown eyes. He was still in the don't-touch-my-hair phase, which drove me wacko. Only during lovemaking was I permitted to run my hands through his tresses, inhale its sweetness, knowing full well that soon would come the shampoo and blow dryer which would transform him into the John Travolta of *Saturday Night Fever* fame. The few times I caved in to temptation and so much as touched his hair as he walked by, I paid for it. How I hated that scowl, that darkness which came over his face, that sharpness in his voice.

With the obvious exception of his hair, Don disliked his body, something I could never understand. He had an aversion to having his picture taken and refused to look in full-length mirrors, confining himself to the bathroom mirror that cut him off just below the waist. He would swivel on the balls of his feet, checking out the top two-thirds of his body from all angles—but only the top two-thirds.

I never tired of looking at him, though. Without realizing it, my eyes often caressed his body with such adoration and longing that he would snap, "Don't look at me like that!" I tried; I really did, but was often unsuccessful. One Wednesday night, as he and Frank were on their way out, it was Frank who did the snapping. I cast one last admiring glance Don's way as he headed out the door.

"Christ, do you have to drool over him like that," Frank snorted, his voice dripping with disgust.

It's not as if Don had no sense of humor about his body. He had what I dubbed a practical penis. When not in use for our favorite pastime, it would shrivel away to a pittance, neatly out of the way. However, when roused, it was more than up to the task. He got a kick out of it, explaining how he'd had the best time at

"Mazola parties," those let's-get-naked-and-jump-in-a-pile-orgies in favor with the younger set . . . or so I was told by Don.

"You know, Deb, I used to get off more on the girls who had seen me in the buff before the action started," his eyes twinkled. He chuckled, recalling the look in their faces and the marked surprise in their voices as he made his entrance into the fray: "Don, is that you?"

Much of the pleasure in our sexual relationship in the early days came from that sense of playfulness. Just about everything we did had a sensuous element to it, even the silliness.

A Sunday morning over plates of bacon, eggs and his famous home fries, turned downright goofy as we tried to top each other with unusual song titles, especially of country songs. Since neither of us was remotely a fan of such music, I was taken aback by his knowledge.

"The best title I've ever heard is *I've Got Tears in My Ears From Lying on My Back in My Bed Crying Over You*," he offered.

"Oh, get out. You made that up," I insisted between peals of laughter.

He stood firm. "Wanna bet?"

"Sure," I replied.

"What do I get when you lose? And you WILL lose."

I got up and poured myself another cup of coffee, tapping the sides of the mug with my fingertips. "Let's see. What would make it interesting? I know. How about I give you a blow job while standing on my head?"

"You're on." He chuckled and headed for the phone to call his dad for proof of his assertion. I could see by the delight in his eyes he thought he had me good.

"Hold it, pal, not so fast. I'm gonna require a little more documentation than that, like a recording or sheet music."

His face fell. From that day on he never missed the opportunity to prove the existence of that song. He popped into every music store we drove past, often turning around or skidding to a quick stop. My luck held, thank God. I hadn't the foggiest notion of how I would have paid off my debt. I never did learn to stand on my head. A decade or so after our relationship ended, I was leafing through some old sheet music in the back of Jack's Music in Red Bank when I saw it. *Sorry pal,* I chuckled to myself, *the statute of limitations ran out on that bet long ago.*

Later that Sunday, with the kids still at Jeff's, we settled into the living room for whatever football game was on the tube. Walking into the room with the usual chips and dip, I was astonished to find Don had made-up the sofa bed. We cuddled together during the game, and wasted no time starting our own traditional half-time ritual.

"Sure is more fun than watching football with the guys," he murmured, his hair tickling my bare belly.

Coming home from an evening out one Saturday, we were almost at our street when the sultry FM voice of Alison Steele, "The Nightbird," made its way over the car radio, introducing a new Donna Summer song.

"Next we have something very special, something I'm not sure how to describe," she crooned. "Let's just say, I don't advise listening to this song in a supermarket."

As we pulled into the driveway, we heard the first strains of "Love to Love You Baby." Don shut off the car. We sat silently for a minute or so, listening to something we had never heard before—at least not over the public airwaves. It was an orgasm set to music. Don grabbed my hand and hustled me into the house, quickly switching on the kitchen radio.

"This is not something to listen to in a car, either," he proclaimed, pulling me close. We stood, swaying softly together as the silken voice wound its way through a series of musical moans, punctuated by murmurs of, "love to love you baby," for what we later learned was a full 17 minutes. We didn't speak or kiss or make love in any conventional sense, but the intensity of emotion flowing between us was enough to light a small city.

He would often interrupt whatever I was doing with "Come here," calling or pulling me into the living room to slow dance to some song or another on the radio, reminding me how my dad would often dance my mother around the kitchen for no particular reason. Only the green lava lamp atop the TV usually lighted the room. He was forever dimming the lights and lighting candles. On Christmas Eve after the children were in bed, he shut off all but the tree lights and we sat sit quietly, sipping a glass of wine and exchanging gifts. Even Halloween took on a new glow.

It was easily the best Halloween of my life, the one I spent with Don that first October. Josh pranced around in an elaborate Superman suit and Lizzie was doll-like as a fairy queen, wand and all. My Aunt Betty had outdone herself that year and surprised us with homemade outfits. But it isn't the trick-or-treat stuff that sticks out most in my memory. It was the "War of the Worlds" broadcast. I bet it's an annual event. That year, however, was the only time I paid it any mind. Don suggested we make a night of it. After the kids were asleep, we climbed into the king-size bed in my crimson bedroom and plumped up the pillows. We had jury-rigged a stereo directly across on the inner wall, the lights were dimmed and candles lit. We huddled together and listened to Orson Welles' infamous broadcast.

I had never before stayed still and really listened to the show. It was wonderful. His deep voice danced up and down my spine much like Don's. Afterwards, we made slow luxurious love before falling into sleep. Don loved to sleep curled up around my back, since actually sleeping with someone was a new experience for him.

"I swear to God, you're like a furnace," he said one chilly night. "You give off so much heat, it doesn't much matter that you hog most of the blanket."

That was when the sex was best, when it grew naturally out of another activity. It wasn't so great if we came at it straight—then I tended to try too hard and it fell flat, especially for him.

To mark the New Year's Eve ushering in 1976, we splurged and went out to eat at a fancy restaurant. But we left before the revelries started, heading out to the beach alone. It was cold but still and ever so silent. The silence was light, though, not oppressive, an anticipatory silence, a cleansing silence. We walked along the jetty in the shelter of the rocks, watching black foaming waves break on the shore. It was one of those nights you can see forever gazing up at the stars, back before time began, before the earth existed. We held hands; we held our breath, too, without realizing why.

Returning slowly to the car, neither of us broke the silence that bound us together, an intimacy stronger than any act of love. Midnight struck as we rounded the Brielle Circle. The road was deserted. Off in the distance, we could hear the muffled sounds of celebration, the soft popping of firecrackers, like hundreds of Champagne bottle corks. A new year had begun. Don stopped the car halfway around the traffic circle, right in the middle of the road and kissed me.

"Let's think about getting married sometime soon, OK?"

"OK," I answered automatically, taken entirely off guard by his proposal. It seemed to come from those distant stars.

"Could we have a baby?" he added, his face soft and solemn.

I took a second to inhale before I could find my voice to answer. *A baby? His baby? Of course we could have a baby.*

"Yes," I said, smiling. "I'd love for us to have a baby."

I was already eating for two, anyway. I loved eating with Don. It was a large part of our relationship. This was another relief from Jeff, who could eat twice his weight but didn't relish food much, with the exception of a good home-cooked Italian meal. Jeff's ability to put it away without it showing drove me bats, and he was six years older than I was.

At 19, Don could also pack it in, and with me almost a decade his senior and female to boot, all this indulgence showed up on me pretty fast. This did not please Don. Although he tended to be attracted to chunky, petite and full figured women, that didn't apply to me. When we met, I was in fighting form, a comfortable size 12. By the time he left I was at least 30 pounds heavier, weight which literally fell off as soon as he was gone.

As my girth increased, I noticed how much attention Don

paid to my body. No man had ever been so concerned or observant. While it was certainly flattering, it was also disturbing in a way I could never put my finger on. It was as if I had somehow lost ownership of my own body. Emerging from the shower one morning, he grabbed a towel and started drying me off.

"Come over here by the light," he said, nudging me closer to the bathroom window. He turned me around, studying my back.

"What's wrong?"

"You're back is all broken out," he answered. "I think you should start washing your hair first instead of last so the oil from your hair won't be the last thing to run down your back."

"Don, that just doesn't make any sense," I reasoned. "The shampoo that's carrying the oil from the hair would do the same for the back."

"Will you just give it a try?" he retorted. "It isn't going to hurt."

So I did it, although my mom had taught me to wash my hair last so I wouldn't catch a chill in the shower. OK, maybe that doesn't make much more sense than my dad telling me not to wear socks to bed or my feet wouldn't grow. It's just hard to change habits like that.

He also hated make-up or artifice of any kind, which was okay with me. Lipstick was the most I felt the need of back then, bras were definitely optional equipment and I was more than content to let my last-washed sable brown hair fall in natural waves to my shoulders. Close to the end of our relationship, when I curled my hair to see how it would look as an afro, he ridiculed me ruthlessly. But it didn't stop me. I cut my hair into a fro and even started wearing make-up.

This proprietary attitude extended toward all his romances. Don couldn't understand why his girlfriends got lean and sexy after he broke up with them and complained about it more than once. I can't speak for them, but with Don and me the answer was plain as day. Eating with him was a joy akin to making love.

He relished his food, licking his fingers and lips, chewing with sensuous concentration. We sat and talked and ate and ate. No wonder I grew plump. I may have introduced him to salads, but that pales in comparison to the joy of eating ice cream out of a soup bowl. Where I came from, ice cream was spooned carefully into a dessert dish, the incredible sinfulness of piling the lush creamy stuff to the top of a soup bowl was almost unbearable, another barrier to pleasure abolished by this beautiful young man. That didn't stop him, however, from pointing out to me sometime later that ice cream was my downfall. Ice cream? No, not ice cream, not Haagen-Dazs chocolate chocolate chip but Donald James DeLuca. He awakened and sharpened all my appetites.

What else? Oh yeah, bacon sandwiches—not a slice or two alongside a couple eggs, like a tasty garnish, to be apportioned carefully so as not to run out of the tasty morsel before the eggs were consumed. Oh no, slabs of the pig slices fried up tender in a pan, not hard and dry, but resilient to the tooth like meat, layered on bread. The first time I came downstairs, lured by the bacon aroma and found him about to chow down, I could hardly believe my eyes. Don had spread at least six slices of bacon out on the bread and was slathering on mayo, salt and pepper. He was humming.

"What the hell is that?" I shrieked.

"A bacon sandwich. Want one?" He licked the extra mayo and bacon grease from his fingers.

"A what?"

"Hey, don't knock what you haven't tried," he said, slicing his creation in two and offering me half.

So I tried—many times.

He tossed franks on the griddle with little cuts so they came out round, much to the delight of the kids. Tomatoes had to be sliced so thin for sandwiches that you could see through the solid flesh. French fries were made from real potatoes and served still greasy, boardwalk style.

It was after one of his late-night fried potato feasts that I awoke from a fitful sleep with a burning sensation in my chest. Convinced it was a heart attack or some other life-threatening seizure, I reached to wake up Don. But as I did, I sat up and the heat subsided for a moment. It hit me. *This was heartburn, my father's chronic ailment.* The realization I was already too old to eat without consequences was akin to stumbling across that first gray hair. I crept out of bed and downstairs for the antacid I kept on hand for my dad, relieved I hadn't awakened Don. I sat in the dark on the couch for a long while, hugging my knees to my chest.

Coffee, which he consumed constantly, contained at least three spoons of sugar and loads of non-dairy creamer. He loved those instant French vanilla café things I introduced him to, but he even added sugar to that. Now I know there is often a relationship between sugar addiction and alcoholism, but being somewhat of a sugar fiend myself, I didn't pay it much mind. Fact is, I don't recall seeing him drink all that much. There was rarely even beer in the house, so he confined his drinking to bars mostly, and I was rarely with him. I wasn't a regular drinker, and it didn't occur to me to have it around. Growing up, we never drank with meals at home and if there was beer in the house, I knew we were having pizza. Booze was for parties or company, at which time my father got loaded and obnoxious. Wine was for Passover.

Bungle in the Jungle

It was a Sunday afternoon in late August, several weeks before Frank was to be married in a typical Catholic shotgun affair. The day was thick with heat and humidity. The house wasn't air conditioned, and I was trying not to move much. The kids were still at their dad's, so I spent my time in the living room hammock reading, creating a soft breeze by swaying slowly. Don had gone out with Frank a little after noon and the house was as still as the summer air.

About 4 p.m., Don burst through the front door. I looked up, startled. He glanced over at my supine form. I was reclining with a pillow under my head, legs spread to keep my thighs from sticking together in the heat. He stood silently in the doorway, a strange grin spreading across his face. Then he strode quickly up to the hammock, took me by the shoulders and tossed me onto the rug. With one arm he pinned me down, stripping off my shorts with the other. I was too stunned to object and something told me not to try to talk. Besides, it was kind of exciting. Even when he had been persistently spontaneous, he had always been so gentle.

Don stood over me for a moment, then dropped his pants and entered me hard. It was fast and a bit painful and sweat ran down his nose and fell onto my face. It was over as abruptly as it began. He got up, pulled up his pants and walked away without a word, leaving me lying half clothed on the living room rug in front of the bare bay window.

It was a bizarre incident, one we would never talk about. After he got up, I lay there for a while, trying to make sense of it. I could tell he had been drinking, but booze alone couldn't account for this. It was out of character, at least out of the character I knew.

When I finally pulled up my shorts and got back into the hammock, I noticed bruises on my upper arms and thighs where he had grabbed me. They hurt when touched, but I kept running my fingers lightly over them, relishing the sensation. A nagging thought at the edge of my mind tried warning me this had its roots in Frank's upcoming nuptials.

Frank didn't like me right from the start. Okay, maybe that's not fair. It's probably more accurate to say at first he didn't dislike me. I was just another chick, another female to serve, fetch and carry, to laugh at his semi-crude and often bigoted jokes. Only I didn't laugh. He was transparent to me. After it became clear that I wasn't some sexual hit and run for Don, his gaze grew hostile and his voice slick, more patronizing. Yet he was unflaggingly, agonizingly polite. Although Don refused to allow Frank's macho shit to get in the way of our relationship growing serious, he also insisted on maintaining their friendship. When he moved in with me and the kids, I thought Frank would explode from keeping his lashing tongue in his mouth. As for me, I was all too aware of Frank's duplicitous nature, how he urged Don toward more drink, drugs and other women.

I tried not to utter petty remarks but was only partly successful. I didn't actively try to come between them because I sensed it was hopeless. But it didn't please me to see them gallivant off to bars together. Frank's casual screwing around on his longtime girlfriend, Annie, bothered me no end. When Don covered for him, I was indignant. More so, because I knew Don really cared for Annie. *How could he do that to her?* I'm sure I was also afraid if he could do it to her, he could do it to me. What was it Don saw in Frank, a shallow, misogynist jerk with no ambition beyond getting drunk, high, laid and working for his father? I wanted to believe Don had nothing in common with him.

When Annie learned she was pregnant, she turned to Don. I arrived home from the supermarket that wet July afternoon startled to find her crying in his arms. I did my best to stay busy in another part of the house, but I was dying to know what was going on. About an hour later, Don came upstairs and confirmed my suspicions. I came downstairs briefly and put my arms around her.

"I'm so sorry, Annie. You know Don and I will do anything we can to help out."

Then I made myself scarce again, realizing full well whom she had come to see. I knew Don was very fond of, even attracted, to Annie. We had joked about it. So when he took her home and didn't return until the next day, a small part of me wondered how much consoling he had done. But I kept my suspicions to myself. To voice them would have given them viability. And while Don went out of his way to comfort her, he was convinced Frank wouldn't cave in to marriage. He was wrong.

A week or so later, Don came home in a foul mood. He brushed past me without so much as a hello, switched on Cat Stevens and settled into the living room in the dark, smoking one cigarette after another. After an hour or so I couldn't stand it anymore and sat down next to him on the couch.

"What's wrong?"

He ignored me. I sat and waited silently for a few minutes.

"For God's sake, Don, you're scaring the hell outta me. What the hell happened?"

"Frank and Annie are getting married."

I smiled. I just couldn't help myself. Don was livid.

"I knew you'd react like that," he yelled. "This is going to be a fuckin' disaster." I reached to comfort him. "Just get the hell away from me."

I, too, thought Annie was making a big mistake. But finally, Frank was being called upon to pay up, to take responsibility. It was sweet. I hoped the marriage would rid me of Frank and his interference in our relationship. I, too, was wrong.

Frank and Annie's wedding was a grand, gaudy, Italian Catholic affair. The stately church overlooked the lake in Spring Lake, where the obligatory wedding photos were shot near one of the wooden footbridges. I recall it was fall, because the next day we met them at a Wall Township High School football game. So much for ridding myself of Frank.

I piled my thick brown hair atop my head. On my feet were cork platform sandals, the only decent shoes I had. It was those shoes that produced a cutting remark from Don's sister when she saw the wedding photos. It was his family's first look at me, the infamous older woman. And my shoes didn't pass muster. I wore a long navy blue Empire waist dress with white polka dots I borrowed from Carin.

I made the trip up to her house in Holmdel a week before the wedding. We hadn't seen much of each other since Don had moved in. She flipped through the dresses in her closet silently, and I could tell by the rigidity of her back she was put out. I waited; sitting cross-legged on her bed, until she turned and tossed a few dresses my way.

"Here, give these a try," she said. " They come to mid-calf on me so they might not drag on the ground. Carin, a long-limbed blonde, was a good four inches taller than I was.

"I'll probably take them up in the width," I remarked.

"You mean in the boobs," she said, trying to smile.

I discarded all but one of the offerings in rapid succession. I hated wearing her clothes. She had one of those elegant bodies, a pen-and-ink drawing. Mine was drawn with chunky magic markers. I felt ridiculous in her things. I sat back down on the bed facing her.

"Are we gonna talk, or what?"

"What's there to talk about?" she shrugged. "You choose to live with that boy."

"That boy . . . you sound like my mother, for Christ sake. You choose to live with Winston, that schmuck. Bobby chooses to live with his wife and screw half the town . . . So everybody gets to choose somebody but me. Is that it?"

"That's not what I . . ." I cut her off.

"What is it about Don and me that gets everyone so steamed . . . that he's not a 36-year-old balding dentist? Or maybe that he takes up my time and attention, that I'm not all that available, that I have my own life for once?"

"We just want you to be happy."

"Damn it. I AM happy . . . I've been happier these past five months than in the five years I was married to Jeff."

"You can't build a life on sex."

"Try building a life without one. I did," I retorted. "Have you any idea how insulting that is? Don't you think more of me than that? Just because I'm crazy for his bod doesn't mean that's all there is to him. Don may be young, but he's also incredibly intelligent, sensitive and perceptive. Why don't you give him—us—a chance?"

"Deborah, you're going to get hurt. He's so damn young."

"Well, it won't be the first time, will it? I'm not that stupid, Carin. I know this probably isn't going to last forever. You're right, regardless of how much we love each other, he's too young to settle down . . . Let me tell you something. I can't imagine a hurt bad enough to make me regret these past five months."

The wedding turned out to be pleasant, although I had girded myself for the worst. With Don as best man, I knew I would be left adrift, to sit among strangers. Yet somehow it blurs in my memory as a bright splash of color. The reception was at Mike Doolans on Route 71, so we didn't have to travel. The weather was pleasantly warm and sunny and Don didn't get obnoxiously drunk until late in the day.

The newlyweds had no honeymoon. I was pushed into seeing them again the next day at that football game, where Frank lavished his attention on Don. Annie looked as unhappy as I felt. A dark shadow, deep behind her eyes, told me she already sensed she had made a mistake. Frank remained more married to Don than to her.

Father and Son

Don answered the phone, spoke briefly and hung up. He walked over and sat down next to me on the couch. I felt his weight on the cushion beside me and put the newspaper aside.

"That was my mom," he said.

"Is something wrong?"

"You tell me. We have an invitation to Thanksgiving."

"We?" I asked.

"Yup."

"I think it's great. How 'bout you?"

"I agree. It's long past time you met the clan, but . . ." he hesitated, "I'm not sure I can handle this with the kids. Do you mind?"

"Not at all . . . They can spend the holiday with their grandparents. This is gonna be tough enough."

For all his adolescent rebellion, Don was a nervous wreck. He wanted very much for his family to like me and accept me, which made me so anxious it was hard to breathe. I can still remember the dark brown, bell-bottomed knit slacks I wore. They were thin with age but the only ones I had that didn't look too shabby. I bet I wore those offensive cork platform shoes, also. I wore them everywhere then.

Naturally, Don had prepped me on family traditions, the groaning board, the jokes, the ritual loosening of the belts at the close of the feast cooked by his mom. The long table was festively set and extended from the kitchen into the small living room of the Seaside Park Cape Cod; a very close fit for a family the DeLuca's size. The décor was unpretentious lived-in Colonial. It was a warm home, and I was made to feel welcome.

It was the all-American Thanksgiving dinner: turkey, sweet and mashed potatoes, stuffing, pies, the works. The only pallid entry was the iceberg lettuce, tomatoes and cucumbers that passed for a salad. No wonder Don thought he didn't much care for salad until he had mine. "I never knew all those things could go into a salad," he exclaimed the first time he watched me prepare some.

I was edgy about eating. Several weeks before I had gone on an all-protein diet. Living on eggs and franks, I had lost about 10 pounds. I knew as soon as those sweet potatoes hit my system it would pile back on. Don wouldn't like that, but I couldn't very well pass up his mom's cooking, either. (The dam broke and I never could get my eating under control again until he moved out. Then I went on a 6-week fast and dropped 30 pounds before tripping across him and some bitch leaving a motel. Diving into a bucket of Kentucky Fried Chicken, I surfaced 35 pounds later.)

Of course, I had heard about his family for months, as much as they probably had heard about me. I was hoping his mom would like me. Don talked about her with such admiration. I loved that he liked his mother. Don was 10 when his alcoholic father abandoned them, leaving Grace alone with three children to support.

He never mentioned his biological father, although he was sure to remember him. Several years into his mom's second marriage, the children took Richard DeLuca's name. Don told me how the decision whether or not to be adopted by Richard was left up to them, how he had struggled with the choice. He never said what his birth name had been, never volunteered any information about his father. I never thought to ask, as if it didn't matter at all. Maybe that's because my own children's father had beamed out of their lives. I didn't realized until after his death, how large his biological father loomed by this very absence of conversation. He lurked behind Don's brown eyes, silent and destructive, quietly seeping into Don's consciousness and poisoning his life.

When his parents split up, they were living in Rochester, New York. Grace and Richard met at the junior college where he taught art and she was studying nursing. It's to his credit that her three children didn't scare him away. Richard, however, never liked me. He was civil but coldness rolled off of him. When I'm feeling generous, I chalk it up to his love for Grace and the grief our relationship may have caused her. Although she was always gracious, I can only guess at her real feelings.

Richard was a small man with an oversized ego, a man of creativity who never realized his full potential. I was sometimes put off by his pomposity, although he had a jovial good nature much of the time and treated my children well. The rivalry between Richard and Don for his mother's attention and affection was palpable. It was obvious Don resented Richard, while at the same time wanted desperately to gain his approval.

Angela, beautiful, smart and lovable, was obviously the apple of everyone's eye. Despite her disapproval of my wedding shoes, it didn't take long for me to warm up to her. I also quickly grew very fond of Nick. In his teens, Josh often reminded me of him, free spirited and irresponsible with undirected musical talent. At least that's the Nick I remember, the boy.

As we settled in to the car for the ride home, weary from a combination of extended tension and way too much food, Don sighed with relief and pleasure.

"So, how'd I do?" I ventured.

"Are you kidding, they were bowled over," he said with a wide grin. "I'm sure they were expecting some over-aged bimbo."

"It was a dark and stormy night. Seven robbers sat in a cave, so bold and brave. And the littlest one said, 'Tell us a story, Cornelius.'" For the longest time, Lizzie and Josh would sit, mesmerized by this enticing narrative. It would continue: "and Cornelius said, 'It was a dark and stormy night. Seven robbers sat in a cave, so bold and brave . . .'" I can't say how many times Don could go through this before the kids would scream for him to stop. In truth, it had the same effect on me, except I never tired of it, never tired of that voice, something between a whisper and a caress, never tired of its cadence, never tired of a story that went nowhere. It mattered not. Don was all.

His "robot" also transfixed the kids, but after a few minutes they grew frightened and begged him to stop. His eyes would glaze over, unfocused; his movements became jerky and rigid. He would slide his feet back and forth, head cocked to side at an odd angle. I loved it, fascinated by his ability to stay in character.

He was so ambivalent in his feeling toward my kids. He loved them and hated them. They were less conflicted. Five-year-old Lizzie didn't care for him. He wasn't Jeff, and she still felt close to her dad although he had been out of the house for half her young life. Josh, at 3, had no memory of living with his dad and quickly became close to Don, although both of the kids naturally resented how he sopped up my attention.

From a practical point of view, having Don around was great for Josh. There's just that guy stuff. I couldn't have very well taught him how to pee standing up, which Don handled with much patience and humor. And the two were often on the same wavelength, with Don recognizing Josh's nascent 3-year-old sense of humor. Josh would put his shoes on the wrong feet for the tenth time in a row, or his shirt on backwards or inside out refusing to follow my instructions.

"Like this, mom," he'd say brightly, once again having screwed it up. Just as I was about to lose it, I'd hear Don chuckle. "He's goofin' on you."

"Don't be silly. He's just a baby." But then I'd see them exchange a glance and the light would dawn.

That first summer Don and I spent an inordinate amount of time in bed with the door locked. I can recall their insistent banging on the door, yelling for us to come out. Much to my regret, I wasn't all that responsive. My first orgasm had been too long in coming and it overwhelmed me with pent-up lust. And being barely 19, Don was more than up to the task at hand.

As the oldest of three, Don had a way with kids. He obviously loved both Angela and Nick, and I spent many an hour listening to family anecdotes. One of his favorites involved Nick's toilet training, often fertile ground for humor in any family unit. When little Nicky would dash about the house in the altogether leaving little deposits around the family would refer to them as "golden nuggets."

My two, though, could confound his efforts in the damnedest ways. There was the infamous peanut butter and jelly sandwich incident, for example. The first time he made one for them he made it wrong and they carried on, refusing to eat it. Instead of spreading the peanut butter on one piece of bread, the jelly on the other and putting the two together, Don committed the unpardonable sin of spreading the jelly atop the peanut butter and covering it with a dry slice of bread. Mon Dieu! No amount of coaxing could remedy the situation, so Don ate the sandwiches himself and made two more for them.

Don took care of the kids while I was in school, and I was very comfortable leaving him in charge. Evidently, he once made them clean up the backyard as punishment for some dastardly offense. To this day, they both remember the punishment but have conveniently forgotten the crime.

He took his responsibility for the children to heart and was not above letting me have it if he felt I had let them down. When Lizzie got sick and threw up all over herself, he wasted no time in cleaning her. But that was just the beginning. He was down on his hands and knees in the bathroom with a scrub brush when I got home from school.

"What happened?" I asked. "Where are the kids?"

"Josh is over at David's house. I put Lizzie to bed, she's sick to her stomach and running a fever." He glared at me.

I checked on Lizzie and sure enough, she was burning up. She dropped off to sleep after I gave her some baby aspirin. Don was still scrubbing down the bathroom.

"I'm sorry, Lizzie always throws up when she starts to get sick. Thanks for taking such good care of her . . . I'll run down the street and get Josh, OK?"

He ignored me.

"Are you angry about something?"

"Your damn right I am. Look at this place. It's filthy!" He kept right on working. "No wonder the kid got sick. Deborah, this has got to change."

After Don made his version of a wedding proposal that New Year's Eve, he began to make more of an attempt to be a father to the kids. My divorce had become final in December and Jeff had departed for parts unknown the day after the hearing. He left to visit his mother in Florida and never returned. That was the last his children heard from him. He didn't even bother to say good-bye. Lizzie was really affected by his abandonment and for years would refuse to say good-bye to anyone. When my parents would come for a visit, she would run upstairs and hide when it was time for them to go–refusing to be coaxed down.

Against such a backdrop, Don had his work cut out for him. Neither of them was in an open frame of mind. To be fair, I'm not sure how full his own heart was. After all, he was not-yet-20 years old. It would have been a difficult situation for a guy twice his age. But he was determined to live up to his image of his adopted dad. Of course, Richard was in his 30s when he married Grace and welcomed her children as his own. No matter, Don was resolute.

One dreary late winter Sunday, Don announced we were going to the Ocean County Mall. With much ceremony, he ushered me and the kids into my Ford Falcon station wagon. We arrived to find one of those craft fairs going on and for a while we all had a pleasant time walking around. When Lizzie insisted on carrying around the $5 I told her she could spend and then promptly lost it, I was furious. She stood there crying while I fumed, I had so little money. But Don took her aside and calmly handed her another $5 bill, assuring the child it was an accident and could happen to anyone. I watched in amazement as she solemnly took the bill from his hand.

"I don't want her to think we don't trust her," he said, as she skipped ahead of us down the mall concourse.

Then Don spotted a booth that did face painting, where a clown was making up kid's faces with outrageous designs. He thought it was a grand idea, but the kids hung back. He persisted. Trying my best to support Don, I urged them to give it a try, even allowing myself to be painted with a rose on my cheek. Lizzie agreed to a small star under her right eye. But Josh started shrieking when the clown came up to him, and I had to carry him away.

Don took it as if he had been the one rejected. Everyone was silent on the way home, except for Josh whimpering in the back seat. He pulled into the driveway, didn't get out from behind the wheel or shut the car off. As soon as the kids and I got out, he peeled out without a word. I fell asleep long before he got home. The next morning he was too hung over to get out of bed.

I didn't understand his need to step in, to prove himself. They had a father. I had no idea he was gone for good back then. Why couldn't Don just relax and enjoy the kids? Unfortunately, my lack of understanding led to gross insensitivity on my part. One rainy day, looking to amuse the kids, I ran old family movies. Of course, Jeff was in them. Happy times, like all home movies, of birthdays and boardwalk carousel rides. I actually thought Don would get a kick out of seeing them as tiny tikes and called him in to the room. What a jerk. It never occurred to me he would be hurt by seeing them with their father. At the time, we didn't know the other existed. He became sullen and when questioned, raged at me before slamming the front door behind him. Another lost night.

A month or so later, the four of us were having dinner at my folks', a rare and always tension-filled experience from the get go. During the course of conversation, Josh slipped and said something about Don punishing him. After some pointed back and forth, it came out that both kids had been stealing change out of his dresser drawer. He had caught and punished them. I was astounded, then incensed. How could this happen without my knowledge? We argued, right there at the table, right in front of my parents, something we had never done before. I felt so betrayed.

"How come you never told me about this?"

"It was between me and the kids," he retorted. "It was none of your business."

The argument escalated in the car on the way home and after Lizzie and Josh were in bed I exploded.

"Look, stealing is very serious. You should have talked to me about it. I'm their mother. You had no right.'

'If I'd have told you about it, you would have intervened," he insisted. "I was trying to build a relationship with the kids. Why couldn't you just leave it alone for once?"

He couldn't understand my rage at being excluded, and worse yet, his encouraging my children to keep secrets from me. To my mind, this was inexcusable. To Don, this was another example of my lack of respect for him. It was as if we were shouting over static filled phone lines. The louder we yelled, the harder it was for us to hear one another.

The photos aren't dated so I can't be sure, but Josh looks to be about four. It's a birthday party for him. The traditional kind we used to throw, with lots of kids, piñatas, pin the tail on the donkey, musical chairs and bobbing for apples. The large metal drum filled with water was on the floor in the den alongside the kitchen. I took photos of the kids with dripping hair as they picked their soaking heads out of the bucket. Don surprised me by plunging in and capturing an apple, taking a hefty bite and then offering it to Josh. He was too busy to notice I was snapping away. They are my favorite photos of him, his hair heavy with water, hanging down, as he pulled himself up, his hair stuck to his cheeks and neck as he offers his prize to my son. Josh was wearing a shirt Don gave him as a gift. It had a monkey on it and the slogan "Get off my back."

Other snapshots of that day, however, tell a more complete story, one of dark looks and the back of his head. He was angry, for what reason I no longer recall. His glare got more intense the more I took his picture. But for some insane reason, I insisted on snapping away, determined to catch him off guard in some joyous moment.

PART II: SILENT SUNLIGHT

I Wish, I Wish

I agonized over leaving him still sleeping on the cold dark mornings as I left for class, his dark hair fanned out on the pillow. I would lean over him and quietly inhale his fragrance as I rose, in a vain attempt to carry him with me as I went about my day. It was harder still to find him sitting in front of the television on the sofa, legs stretched out on the cedar chest when I returned late in the day. The restaurant where he worked had closed for the season and he seemed unable or unwilling to find another job, I was never quite sure which. I only knew that any suggestion I made, regardless of how gentle or tactfully couched, was enough to a provoke a sneer to a scene.

He would inevitably be wearing his navy blue thermal jacket over a bare torso. Sometimes the hood would be pulled up, shading his face from all but a front view. Chain-smoking Marlboros, he stared blankly at the TV screen, sipping overly sweetened and creamed coffee. His feet, clad only in socks, were crossed at the ankles and rubbed rhythmically back and forth, wearing holes in the tops of his socks instead of the usual bottoms. He would ridicule shows like "Bowling for Dollars" in a caustic voice. I never knew if he was stoned or not. With Don, it was often hard for me to tell.

That's probably why I didn't notice his drinking, because back then it didn't seem to affect him nearly as much as the heavy cigarette and pot smoking. He was always rolling joints. I can see him sitting at the kitchen counter crumbling the buds into the top of boxes, tilting it and rolling over the crushed buds with a small piece of paper or cardboard until the seeds collected along the bottom. Then he'd roll plump joint after joint between his thumbs and forefingers, lining them up on the counter.

My capacity for both drinking and pot smoking was notoriously small. One drink, especially with bubbles, and I was feeling real fine. It was the same with pot. A few hits off a joint and I went into a stupor, unable to study or pay attention to the kids. So often I would pass when he offered me one of his creations.

"As soon as you smoke a joint you want to eat or screw, either of which brings you back down," Don insisted one winter afternoon. "You don't like being high." It sounded more like an accusation than an observation.

"That's not true," I shot back. "I also love listening to music when I'm stoned. I can feel the notes pass over my skin." To be fair, though, he may have been on point. I really feared a loss of control back then and a slightly spinning head would frighten me, so I limited myself to two drinks when we went out. He hated that, also. Anything less than equal, enthusiastic participation on my part in his chosen activity was taken as criticism of his behavior.

Of course, most of Don's bar life was lived without me, so I didn't see how much he consumed. Several times a week he would go out with Marc or more likely, Frank. Those were the days of disco and Don did so love to dance, but I'm sure now that drinking was his main recreation. Most of the time I didn't mind staying home with the kids. I was never very fond of bars, and Frank and I were oil and water.

Was it strictly a matter of the decade between us? I don't think so. Bars were never something I took to, especially not as a place to spend the night. I almost always came out more lonely and depressed than when I went in. Going in with someone is different but the smoke, noise and crowds always got to me quickly. Not to Don, but of course the booze had a hold on him, a strangle hold.

Don loved to play games—board games, card games, mind games. He never tired of them; becoming obsessed, addicted perhaps? He would insist we play the same game ad nauseum. As the winter closed in, it got worse. It might have been a sign of depression; I'll never know. He became particularly attached to the backgammon set and would goad me constantly about playing. Eyes shiny, he rolled the dice cup back and forth rhythmically as we sat at the kitchen counter. I can still hear the rattling. He was hard, competitive and enjoyed beating me.

I'm not overly into games of that kind, never have been. Competitive games bring out the ugly side of people, me included. It's a failing of mine, I suppose, in this society that I avoid such situations. I didn't as a kid. I can remember hours of board games at the marbleized gray and pink kitchen table with those shiny chrome legs. Long Sunday afternoons with my family, spent absorbed in the likes of Racko, Monopoly, Scrabble, Parcheesi. The memories are pleasant. When did competing, winning, become uncomfortable? I can't recall.

I believe Don enjoyed playing games with me so much because he could beat me, sometimes through superior skill, but mostly because he wanted it more, wanted it desperately. When I would win at backgammon, we would have to play again and again. It began to bore me, so I would try and slack off just enough to let him win but not so he would notice. I wasn't always successful.

"What the hell are you doing?" he'd snap after I had miscounted the points on the board or some other equally stupid move. "Pay attention, will ya."

I've never been smart enough to play stupid convincingly.

Anyway, I've always regarded backgammon more as a game of luck with the dice, a crap shoot, unlike chess or even Scrabble which depend much more on skill and strategy. He never could get me to play chess, though. I don't enjoy thinking that far ahead. We did have some hot games of Scrabble, and as long as they stayed good-natured I enjoyed them. Occasionally, I would give in to my need to win and then the game became something else, something much less benign.

There was one major upside to all the games, especially gin rummy. It gave me the chance to look at him unobserved. He was intent on the cards, picking them up, fanning them out, rearranging and discarding them. Chills would literally run up and down my spine watching those elegant hands go through the motions. I was so intent on what he was doing I often gave short shrift to my hand—of cards, that is. No wonder he won so often.

He was equally passionate about a few TV shows, Star Trek and Happy Days, an unusual combo. He was among the first of the Trekkies, deep into the philosophical differences between Kirk, Spock and Bones, the lessons in morality and the physical layout of the Enterprise. He talked about how hard it was to come up with common items—like salt and peppershakers—which were futuristic but still recognizable to us 20th century folk. I learned more about fazers, communicators and tricorders than any one person has a right to know. For example, he proudly pointed out that the first communicators were electric razors.

Cool stuff, for sure, but I liked the show better when communicators were from tomorrow and not today's grooming aids. Here again, a stark difference in our basic nature. I liked books, plays and stories with happy or at least upbeat hopeful endings and thought "Gone With The Wind" should have ended a page earlier, with Scarlet running home to Rhet. I argued that fiction should be better than life, that if I wanted realism I could read the newspaper. He scoffed at this, extolling the virtues of romantic tragedy. Our story became one he would have probably chosen to read.

Happy Days, on the other hand, brought into focus the decade difference in our ages. To me, it was a cute show, but not particularly retro. Being born in the late 1940s, it was hard for me to think of the 1950s as the old days as Don did.

Where music was concerned, Cat Stevens was his love. Not only the music, with its unabashedly romantic existential lyrics, but the man himself, down to how he caressed the mike as he sang. Then again, there was Jethro Tull, alternately musically complex and downright macho crude. Come to think of it, not a bad description of Don. I must say, he did get a kick out my thinking that Jethro Tull was a person instead of a band.

The movie version of the Sound of Music was also among his favorite things, a fact I found hard to swallow. When a promo for the movie appeared on TV one night, and he went on and on about how fantastic it was, about how it was his favorite movie, I thought he was putting me on. Although it had been out for a decade or so, I had never bothered to see it, assuming it would be too saccharine for my taste. And knowing how dry his sensibilities were, I was downright shocked at his attraction to the sugarcoated version of Van Trapp family history, not to mention the lilting score. Edelweiss, he proclaimed raptly was the best song. How to reconcile Edelweiss with Aqualung? The complexity, contradictions and layers of personality likely went a long way toward my fascination—as well as my aggravation—with the lad. Regardless, it took some effort for him to convince me to watch it with him on the tube. He was right; it was enchanting. But the damage had been done.

When he asked me if I liked Cat Stevens, the night he first came to dinner, I lied. I wasn't that into artists, just their music. But I had heard someone say they liked him until the Foreigner album, so I repeated it. It was a very un me thing to do, not a good sign. Not too long after, I fessed up. Don didn't mind; rather, he delighted in introducing me to The Cat. Many of our best, and later my worst, hours were spent with his tunes. After we split, I couldn't stand the sound of Cat Steven's voice, and upon learning Don had died, it was the first thing to which I turned. On the way to the funeral, I played "Teaser and the Firecat" over and over. So why I was ambushed by the very same music in the church, I'll never know. His family obviously had the same reaction as I did.

It's as if Don's soul piggybacks onto Cat Stevens' voice, wraps itself around his sound, and penetrates my body as if we were making love—or making war.

As time passed, Don spent an increasing number of hours steeped in coffee and Cat Stevens. He buried himself in science fiction, especially "Dune" by Frank Herbert. As he read, he entered the desert world of Arrakis, created by Herbert, and insisted I come along. I didn't want to and am not sure why. I always loved science fiction, and I enjoyed listening to him rattle on about the book: melange, the mystical spice; the fremen, fierce natives of the desert planet; stillsuits, worn to recycle the body's moisture; and of course, the huge desert worms, large enough for a battalion of warriors to ride. Still, I put off reading it until he finally erupted.

"I don't understand why you won't even try it," he said, shaking with anger. "It's so insulting. You have no regard for my opinion. You think I'm just some dumb kid."

"I had no idea it meant so much to you," I replied, shocked by the rage in his voice. "Of course I'll read it."

I loved and lost myself in it, eventually reading all the sequels. But it only added to the pile of hurts he was accumulating, and I don't think he ever forgave me for not "respecting him enough." It wasn't one of my more sensitive moments.

Like much of what we had together, though, Dune resonates through my life. I have returned to it many times. And often, when people thank me for something I've done, without even thinking, I respond with mock seriousness: "I live to serve," the motto of the superhuman and mystical Bene Gesserit, a order of female monks from Herbert's world. Sometimes, when facing something scary, I silently repeat to myself the book's Litany Against Fear: *I must not fear. Fear is the mind killer. Fear is the little death that brings total obliteration. I will face my fear. I will permit it to pass over me and through me. And when the fear has passed, I will turn my inner eye to see fear's path. The fear will be gone. Only I will remain.*

The Litany came in handy as I was recovering from a bad chest cold that developed a hacking cough. Don had some left over cough syrup from a previous bout with the same bug, so I took some. About a week later I felt the first ominous twinge in my lower gut. It had been some time, but I recognized it instantly. It felt something like a labor pain, a short stabbing sensation that could easily be mistaken for a stomach virus. When the attacks first began I was married only a few months. Innocent twinges became sharp pains that left me bend over in agony; the pains became cramps that over a period of hours would send me to the toilet time and again with no result. After hours of this, hard stools would start, then diarrhea. I would spend what seemed like days on the toilet in a cold sweat, moaning and crying until I was completely empty.

Once I almost passed out from the pain. Exhaustion and long hours of dead-like sleep would follow. Then I would be fine until the next episode, days, months or years later.

Test of all kinds proved negative, dietary changes had little or no effect, although over the years, I discovered an episode could sometimes be triggered by ice cream. I learned to recognize the signs early and head home to wait out what I knew was to come. My husband was sympathetic but helpless, as was the medical profession. They labeled it a "functional problem," meaning they could find no organic cause, "spastic colon" they said, a benign form of colitis. Learn to deal with stress, they said. Eat more fiber, they said, prescribing muscle relaxants that sent me to the moon, not a bad feeling I must admit. Eventually, I discovered that if I worked back about a week I could almost always identify an emotional trigger or an event that set things in motion. I learned to live with–or rather around—what is now called IBS, irritable bowel syndrome. After my husband and I separated, it disappeared as suddenly as it had arrived.

Now it was back; I was sure of it. I thought back a week and could find nothing upon which to hang it, until I remembered the cough syrup. Oh shit, I grabbed the bottle and read: Codeine. Once I had been given codeine for pain and it had brought down my colon in a big way. I had forgotten. I looked at my watch, 4 p.m. Okay; I had some time before it got real bad. Hopefully Don would be back home then. By 9 p.m., I was shaking in pain, alternating between curling up on my bed and sitting on the john trying to force the inevitable. I knew the pain wouldn't stop until I expelled it all and wanted to get it over with, regardless of the immediate cost. I strain. Nothing happens except another spasm. It always reminded me of labor. I could bring on a cramp almost as the doctor could trigger a contraction. It had a similar rhythm, peaking and subsiding. I often used my Lamaze training to control the pain. But unlike labor, of course, there was nothing to show for it in the end, no reward for the labor, just the knowledge it would happen again.

That day it took a very long time. Don took charge of the kids. After they went down for the night, he turned his attention to me. At first, it was hard for me to have him around. Pain strips one of any pretense of dignity. It was embarrassing. But he was a rock, much as my husband had been during labor. I knew that my ex's strength and comfort during those times led me to fall in love with him again and kept our marriage going years after it should have ended. It was the same with Don. He was growing distant, staying up late and not coming to bed, lost behind clouds of smoke and walls of music. The "coffee and Cat Stevens syndrome." Sex was scarce. I was helpless to get close to him, but seeing me unraveling brought him back.

His tenderness and strength amazed me. When it got really bad, he sat on the tub across from me and held my hand, cooing softly and wiping the sweat as it ran down my face. This time though, it was pain without end. I'm still not clear on what happened, exactly how things transpired. But suddenly I was on a stretcher being wheeled into the hospital emergency room. Don told me later I passed out in his arms as I tried to stand up. He called a neighbor to stay with the kids, put me in the car and took me to the emergency room himself. Loss of fluids, they told us, and kept me for 24 hours.

My memory of that night, of the love and concern in his eyes as he held my hand in that closet of a bathroom, nourished me for some months, even as our life together curdled.

Trouble

I could never roll joints to his satisfaction. He tried and tried to teach me, but I was intimidated and fucked it up terribly, especially if he was watching. I would take the paper, lay it out in my hand, sprinkle it with some pot—rarely generously enough according to him—put in some more and attempt to roll it with my thumb and forefinger the way I saw him do it, then lick the open end to seal it, wetting the ends for good measure. It almost never worked. It was like eating with chopsticks, another simple procedure I have never been able to master. If the joints held together at all, they burned badly, unevenly. I did better with the little red plastic roller, but he mocked me for having to rely on a crutch. I tried to take it in good humor, to suck it in, but the ridicule stung, especially if Frank was around, which he often was.

He also made merciless fun of my singing, something I had grown up enjoying. Everybody sang around my house, and I had even sung in public as a child. My mom sang as she did the housework, and we all sang during car trips, full out. To add insult to injury my children egged him on. In the car, for example, if I so much as started humming, Don would reach over and turn on the radio. I took it so much to heart, that I stopped singing at all for many years.

My laugh was often another opportunity for ribbing. It's kind of unusual. Sort of like a hysterical machine gun, or so I've been told. Since my own mother had one of those loud, deep belly laughs from which I suffered incredible humiliation at public functions as a youth, I was aware of controlling my laughter when out with my own children. But at home or among close friends, I relaxed and let go, a bit at least. Don rarely missed a chance to join my kids in poking fun. That Thanksgiving I met his family, Don told me on the ride home that his brother had commented on my weird laugh.

"And you know what, for a minute I didn't know what he was talking about," he smiled broadly. "I'm so used to it." God, how I loved him at that moment. How I wished those moments would last.

The day of my college graduation hangs in my memory, weighed down by expectations and compounded by unbelievably hot May weather. An equally hot, stiff wind did nothing to help. I was relieved to graduate finally at 29 but had no idea where to go from there. A day more of endings than beginnings, of little joy and much anxiety, it was the last time I donned the traditional cap and gown. I did it to please my folks. I despise graduation ceremonies and my own children were a bit young to be more than bored to tears.

My folks presented me with a pair of coffee mugs in the college parking lot. They had already sprung for a white Datsun, after the gas tank literally fell out of my station wagon the preceding month. Don gave me a Cross pen and pencil set. The first decent pen I ever had. The pencil is long gone but the pen survives, although it's rarely used. The act of holding it in my hand evokes his presence. The photos of us together that day are the only ones of the both of us. Taken by my dad in the formal gardens of Monmouth College in Long Branch, they resemble wedding photos. I'm even wearing a white dress and real high-heels.

After the ceremony, Don and I went to a small party at an old farmhouse in Wall Township where fellow graduate Jean, a generously sized blonde, lived with Ted, a stocky bartender with a hair-trigger temper. Our hostess was renowned as a gourmet cook and each dish on the buffet was more exotic and sensuous than the next. It almost overcame the cramped quarters and the stifling heat. I remember Don calling me over to the coffeepot and pointing to a small pitcher in awe: "real heavy cream" he whispered in disbelief.

It was heaven; it was hell. All that remained between us was a flatness, like the flat sweet taste of soda opened too long ago. No matter how hard you screw the top down, the fizz escapes. Soon there is only a faint hint of the carbonation, the bubbles, the life. Regardless of Don's physical presence, he wasn't there, and I couldn't pretend it was all right no matter how hard I tried. And boy, did I ever try. He went through the motions but there was little passion. The day ended very early and, although my folks had the kids, we didn't go anywhere, make love or even sit and talk upon our return to the house. Hollow, I felt hollow and more alone than when he wasn't there. At least then the fantasy, the daydream, was three dimensional and passionate.

If I had been paying attention I would have realized that graduation day marked an end for Don and me. But I was wrapped up in myself, in the relief and terror of graduation after all these years. What was I going to do with a psychological degree from a small local college? How was I going to support the kids? I walked around in a haze.

It wasn't until after his death 20 years later that a slice of understanding penetrated the fog of my brain. Of course, that would have been the last straw. I was now a college graduate. A year had gone by with us together, and he had made no progress. He hadn't written anything substantial, gone back to school or even taken a class. He must have felt he was losing himself in my life, caring for my children while I made my mark. That wasn't the way I saw it of course, but that makes no never mind to the person whose head wrings with hopelessness. He had been out of high school two years, having left his teen years behind. My noticing might have made the passage easier for both of us but would have done little to change the outcome.

Two weeks after my graduation I awoke to him sitting on the edge of the bed watching me, a look of quiet misery on his face.

"My Love, I need to get away," he began, the words spilling

out in a rush. "I am as frightened of your strength as I am attracted by it. I don't know who I am. I'm not you and don't know how to be me. I'm starting to hate the kids. I don't want to be their father; I don't want to be *anyone's* father yet. I don't want to hurt them or you. I don't want to go, but I can't stay. I'll be leaving as soon as I can find a place to go and the courage to get there. I love you and don't want to lose you, but this is something I have to do for me. I know you understand and hope that some day you can forgive me."

I opened my mouth to speak, but he gently placed his fingers to my lips.

"I hope like hell you will still be here when I have worked this all out. I can't imagine my life without you. You've given me so much and deserve to be happy. But there is no way I can make you happy until I can figure out how to make myself happy."

We held each other for a long time. Then he kissed my forehead and went downstairs. I lay in bed for the better part of the morning, unable to pull myself together. When I finally walked downstairs, I was outwardly calm. I poured myself some coffee and faced him across the kitchen counter. I could hear the kids outside in the backyard.

"Since you feel you must do this, please leave quickly," I said softly. "I can't live under this tension anymore. If this doesn't end soon there will be nothing left for you to come back to."

The following week I dropped him and his possessions back at his parent's house, almost as I had picked him up a little more than a year before. Don choked back tears, silently watching in disbelief as I made small talk with his mom at the kitchen table. He couldn't know how desperately I clung to the numbness, an emotional paralysis that had set in following his bedside declaration of independence. After I'd drained my tea and could delay no longer, I rose to leave.

"I'll walk you to your car," he said, jumping to his feet. He collapsed in sobs against the car window. "Oh, God. I miss you already."

"Go inside, babe, it's getting chilly."
"Drive carefully. Good-bye."
"I will. Good night.'

I managed to hold myself together until the next day, driving the kids home from their dad's. As I pulled into the driveway, I felt no sense of the usual homecoming; stark desolation leered at me. I tried to hustle the kids in the house, to push the feeling aside, but Josh would not be rushed. He insisted on ringing the doorbell, refusing to believe there was no one inside. As the echoing of the bell died down, I opened the front door and found myself unable to move. I was more than numb; I was frozen. The kids playfully pulled me across the threshold, assuming I was joking around. I told them they could watch TV in my bedroom and would bring up some popcorn as a special treat. As soon as they scampered upstairs, I collapsed against the door in sobs.

Less than a week later, Don took a job on the boardwalk in Seaside Heights. A month after that, he bought an ancient white Plymouth Duster complete with the little red devil on its rear and moved into a motel on Route 37 in Toms River.

Maybe You're Right

Pens were important to Don. He realized how a swiftly flowing, easy gripping pen could make writing almost a joy. Such things mean a lot to him. He chose a medium point ballpoint pen. He had done enough writing at the tender age of 19 to form definite preferences. He chose his notebooks with equal care, insisting on narrow, college lined spiral bound books in which to write in his tightly controlled and beautiful hand. To this day, the first thing I do when I pick up a pen is scribble: *does this write*; or *ink flows*. Don's way of testing out a pen to see if it had juice left.

Ink did flow for Don when I knew him. Although he didn't write as such when we lived together, he did keep an extensive and emotional journal. Much of it was written after he moved out, living in a sparse, tiny motel room the size of a large walk-in closet. Once, when his car broke down, he called and I gave him a lift back there. The room was maybe 8x8, smaller than my kids' rooms, and the double bed took up most of it. I sat in a hard chair, the only seat besides the bed where he sat cross-legged, opposite a black and white portable television with rabbit ears.

"I've got a couple of short stories in the mail," he said, sounding upbeat. "Wish me luck."

We chatted for 15 minutes about nothing. I left sad and alone after a small soft kiss on the cheek. He was trying to distance himself from me, but I refused to accept it, not on a gut level anyway. I needed him so. While I made a real effort to support his independence movement, inside I was sick at heart.

By August we had been separated for more than a month. I was unemployed and alone. The kids were spending the month in Connecticut with my aunt and uncle. It was Saturday night, and

I had nothing to do. No one was around. The air stuck to my body. There was no breeze. Just breathing was work. I climbed into the Datsun and started driving around aimlessly, stopping a few times at local watering holes. The music was unbearable loud, the summer crowds claustrophobically dense. Restless, I jumped back into the car and drove. Almost without realizing it, I found myself heading south on Route 35, toward Seaside and Don.

Even at 10 p.m. the boardwalk was teaming with people, a cacophony of color and sound. I hated it. Clusters of city people drinking and shooting a variety of implements at an equal variety of targets to win prizes worth a fraction of what they were spending. I was swimming in a sea of whining children and young lovers shyly holding hands or furiously making out on the dark sand outside the arc of the boardwalk lights. It was a foreign country. I'd lived at the shore for more than a decade and avoided the boards in season, most particularly rowdy Seaside, confining myself to Point Pleasant Beach kiddy rides with Lizzie and Josh on weeknights. But that night, I didn't care. I didn't care that it cost a fortune to squeeze my car into a distant parking space. I was empty and desperate for attention and affection, even though I knew it would cost me dearly.

I found Don hawking a game in which you forked over a quarter to pitch little round plastic discs at frogs on lily pads. Knock off three frogs to win your choice of tiny stuffed animals. I hung back and watched his performance for quite a while, unnoticed. He was in his element, coaxing teasing and seducing one and all, his eyes just a shade too bright. He smiled broadly when he saw me and turned his full pitch my way. I caught on and entered the game immediately, relieved at his reaction.

"You there, young lady, you look like someone with good coordination. Come on, try your luck; take a chance. It's only a quarter, ten chances for a quarter. With a smile like yours, you could charm these frogs right off their little pads. No problem."

I pretended to be reluctant, unsure and a bit shy and let him coax me into playing. We made a good team, a small crowd gathered.

"Come on folks, step up and cheer the little lady on."

I could have used some of that good cheer later on.

"If you wanna hang around, I'll be off at 12," he said, handing me my choice of a little stuffed kitty he had arranged for me to win.

At midnight we walked down to one of the bars dotting the boardwalk. By the 3 a.m. closing time the boards were dark and almost deserted, except for the small cleaning crews emptying wastebaskets and sweeping up debris. I was worn out and struggling against a sinking sadness. It had been a long dreadful night in yet another dingy, noisy bar. Still, I fought against its end. Don was pulling me toward some after-hours joint, but I planted my feet at the door. I'd had enough. He reached into his pocket.

"Here," he said, stretching out an open palm. Glancing down I saw the black capsule, a Black Beauty. I hated amphetamines. Years ago, when I had taken diet pills I detested the rapid, loud beating of my heart.

"Come on. It'll make you feel better. I promise."

I reached over and took the offering, swallowing it down without benefit of water. It delivered as advertised. I made it through in relatively good humor having fooled my body into thinking it was enjoying itself. It was daylight before we parted. The boardwalk, reborn for another day, shone in the early morning light, the same morning light glistening off the parking ticket on my windshield.

When I got home I was keyed up to the point of mania and paced for hours until I started to crash. Alone and panicked, I called Don, but he was in no mood to talk.

"Just take it easy," he said, the irritation in his voice spilling over the phone line into my ear. "You'll feel better in a few hours."

"But . . . but, I'm so scared. I don't know what to do."

"There is nothing to do. What the hell do you want from me?" He hung up hard and loud in my ear.

Abandoned, I curled up on the floor in a dark corner of my

bedroom wrapped in a quilt, sobbing and shivering in the heat, until the next morning.

He called me a week later as if nothing had happened.

"Hey, I just heard that Sears is holding interviews tomorrow at the Holiday Inn in Toms River for the new store. I thought you might want to go down."

"Yeah, I'll go down. Thanks for letting me know." I didn't mention our last conversation.

I scored in the top two percent on Sears employment exam and was among the first hired in the personnel department. I made sure that Don made the cut. He landed in automotive. We saw each other at work and occasionally afterwards, but I was never sure of our status. The chemistry between us remained palpable, though, and it didn't take our coworkers long to consider us a couple—which oddly didn't appear to bother Don a bit.

The weather that winter was dreadful, unusually bitter cold mixed with heavy snow. By then I had been promoted into the management-training program and with the Christmas rush over we were into inventory. I had the flu over New Years Eve and spent it alone in a haze of fever on the living room couch. The kids were with their grandparents for the holidays. All I remember is isolation and illness. The weather and my separation from Don didn't help. I hated my job and without him, life was barren.

At the store's Christmas party, Don had been unusually attentive and I had really enjoyed myself. He had even cut in when Brandon Vorbach, the store manager asked me to dance. We joked on the ride home that Mr. Vorbach looked none too pleased. But it turned out not to be that funny. A few weeks later he called me into his office.

"Deborah, I've been going over your supervisor's notes and find your work is not up to par. If I don't see marked improvement in the next month or so, I'm going to have to drop you from the program."

I hated the job, but still I was stunned, speechless. This was the first time in my life I'd been told I couldn't cut it.

"You might take the time to start looking around for something else, someplace you would be happier," he added. Leaning back in his black leather chair, he tapped the edge of the desk with a pencil. Then he made an almost offhand crack.

"You may want to rethink some of your workplace relationships, also. Someone in a management training position must be aware of whom they are socializing with."

I was beyond furious.

"Excuse me, but when I agreed to join the management program, no one told me this place had non-fraternization rules like the army. Whom I socialize with is my own business." I stood up to leave, not waiting to be dismissed. "Oh, by the way, Don and I have been together since before they broke ground for this place."

I stormed out of his office, knowing I was on borrowed time.

That morning it snowed again. I pushed myself into going to work. The store was closed, either due to the weather or inventory. I am not sure. Anyway, I decided to swing by the Point Pleasant Beach motel where Don now lived, telling myself that maybe he needed a ride to work. As I approached the motel, his car was in front of me. I honked. He pulled over and stopped, and I started to get out to talk to him. Before I had a chance, he all but trotted to my driver's window and we had a strange, tense chat. Later that day, relating the incident to my friend Diane at work, she kept staring at me, wide-eyed.

"Why are you looking at me like that?"

"Are you really that thick or has that guy got you so turned around you can't think straight anymore?"

"What the hell are you talking about?"

"There was woman in the car," she insisted. "Some poor thing he pushed to the floor so you wouldn't see her. That's why he jumped out and ran over."

"Why would he do that? We're both free to see anyone we like."

"Maybe he wanted to spare your feelings . . . or maybe he was just trying to avoid a scene."

Not one to take a hint, sometime soon after I dropped by

again unannounced. He may have extended some vague invitation I took to heart. The room was much larger and nicer than his first and had a table and chairs, a hot plate and small refrigerator. Glancing at the table as I walked in, a hot stab shot through my body.

"I see you've been entertaining," I said, making a futile attempt at sounding light and casual.

He followed my eyes. The remains of food from a nearby McDonald's included a kids meal.

"Oh, that was just Linda. You know, the little redhead who works part time in customer service. I gave her a ride home the other day, so she stopped by with dinner as a thank-you. Her little boy, Evan, was with her."

This was intended, I'm sure, to add a wholesome touch, with a toddler present they weren't messing around. But it had the opposite effect. *He was intimate enough with another woman to be getting to know her child, her child!* One of the main reasons we separated was his discomfort with the papa surrogate role, or so he had said. I was hurt beyond words, but I choked it back, grateful just to be spending time with him. He and I were not having sex at the time. Then, of course, I chalked it up to the little Lindas of this world.

By the time he called me a day or so later, I had mustered up my courage.

"Listen, I can't handle things the way they are," I declared. "Either move back in and be with me and the kids or we're through. I won't see you at all . . . It's up to you."

I hung up before he could respond, believing I would never see him again. My hands were shaking and the receiver was wet with tears. But less than 24 hours later, I answered the door to find him there. He was in shirtsleeves, oblivious to the single-digit temperature, eyes red-rimmed. I threw the door open and pulled him inside, but backed away and sat on the stair level with his eyes. I waited; sure he had come to say a final farewell.

"I want to come back," he croaked, in a voice hoarse from too many cigarettes. "I was up all last night. I want to try again, fresh, to be a family if that's what you want."

I nodded but still didn't move. This was so unexpected it frightened me a little. He took several steps my way and knelt on the stair below me, running his hands over my hair, as if reassuring himself I was really sitting there. He cupped my chin in his hands and gazed intently into my eyes. My tears ran down onto his upturned palms.

"God, I love you. You are my connection to the world, to life. The thought of not seeing you, I just couldn't take it."

Both of us were amazed, I think, at how fast things deteriorated. There were long, self-conscious silences where there had been effortless conversation. He would disappear for long periods of time, offering no explanation. My casual inquiries were met by surly responses. I was so overwhelmed by having him back that I bathed in his presence, walking gingerly around his erratic behavior.

We had been back together for about a month when we had the strangest blow-up. The door to the bedroom was closed and he was haranguing me about something. Sex, I'm pretty sure that was it. For a change, it was me who wasn't interested. He was battering me with his voice, way beyond the usual cutting remarks. I was sitting on the edge of the bed and he was standing over me, yelling. Just before the argument, he had given me a $20 bill, repayment for money I'd laid out for him. I absentmindedly reached for the bill on the bed where he'd thrown it, and it was gone. Still crying, I tore the bed apart looking for it, even crawled on the floor, but couldn't find it. All the while he was following me around berating me, adding this to the litany of complaints.

"How could you be so stupid as to lose $20 right here in the bedroom?" He whipped me into such a frenzy that I missed the obvious. I folded up, growing smaller and smaller until he could hold me in the palm of hand. He had to have put the money back in his pocket and was enjoying the whole scene.

Less than 24 hours later he decided to hang shelves in Lizzie's room. I was pleased but stunned at his sudden turn-around in mood.

"She's getting older," he said. "I want her to have a nice place to bring her friends. They'll be spending a lot more time in her room."

In between harangues and sullen silences, he appeared determined to build a family life. When Lizzie and Josh were in a talent show at school, he not only went with my folks and me but invited his parents. We even talked about seeing a counselor, about getting married. I couldn't get my balance.

So I was already in pretty bad shape when I lost my job. Knowing the ax is on its way down doesn't stop it from smarting when it strikes. I sat in the middle of the mall, hysterical, as Diane tried to calm me down.

"It's not as if you're all alone," she said, stroking my hair. "You still have Don."

"No, I don't. Now that my job is gone, he won't be around much longer, either. Don't ask me how I know. I just do. Lord, how I hate April."

Wild World

The spring weekend Don's friend Joe arrived from upstate New York I thought things might turn around. Joe and Don had been friends since childhood, and Don was beside himself with joy when he arrived. I packed the kids off for the weekend so there would be no distraction, nothing to divert Joe's attention from Don and leaving me free to participate. I fully expected the duo to spend much of their time alone together, but I was unprepared for the events that followed.

Joe was very tall, almost 6' 5," with dark blond curly hair and blue eyes. He towered over Don. Despite his clean-cut good looks, though, Joe was as into drugging and boozing as Don. Much to my dismay and disappointment they lost little time in getting down to it big time. Don pulled down a small mirror from the upstairs hall and dumped some white powder on it, which he chopped at with a razor blade. They did the whole nine yards rolled in a $1 bill and snorted it down. This was a far cry from pot smoking, and even that had become too constant for my comfort. I simply couldn't believe my eyes and yanked Don aside.

"Is that coke? Are you crazy?" I demanded, my voice rising. "You may think me a mental midget where drugs are concerned, but even I know cocaine when I see it."

"Don't be ridiculous," Don scoffed. "It's just THC."

"THC?"

"The active ingredient in pot, the stuff that gets you high," he smirked patronizingly. "It just looks like coke."

And I bought it. I was growing so desperate to keep him from drifting out of my reach, I would have swallowed anything.

About 3 p.m. that Saturday, the pair decided to drop in at

The Cove, a local bar just a few blocks down the road. I was delighted when Don asked me to come along. I didn't care. I was included; we were together. I would put up with anything for that. The bar was dark and cool, sparsely populated and there was no loud head-banging dance music that time of day. Encouraged by Don, I drank a bit more than usual and was feeling high and fine when the three of us headed back to the house by 7 p.m. I looked forward to a pleasant evening. Don was uncharacteristically amorous and danced me upstairs. The lovemaking was vigorous, especially on his part, and I started to release the rest of my anxiety. But as soon as he was satisfied he shot out of bed and got dressed.

"Where are you going?"

"Joe and I are going out," he answered, making it clear I wasn't invited.

I was shattered. The whole day had been a ruse, a game on his part, to get me drunk and out of the way so he could have the night free for real fun with Joe. I felt dirty and used. Even the lovemaking now seemed forced, as if he needed to booze and coke up before he could touch me. I protested only mildly, I'm ashamed to say. But he flew into a rage anyway at my "clinging and demanding nature." Even though I knew I had been set up, it didn't matter. I was broken and alone. He stumbled back into bed about 4 a. m. Wherever he and Joe went, they had obviously spent the night. He was beyond drunk. He reeked from sweat and liquor, and I turned away from him. He didn't notice. After a few minutes, he vomited all over the pillow.

The next day we barely spoke. He busied himself enjoying his last hours with Joe. I took a lot of Polaroids that day of the two of them for Don, and of just him, for myself. Instead of turning his face from the camera as usual, he mugged it up and posed and never said a word about it. It was odd, and I knew it. I still have several of those photos, the one with Don and Joe arm in arm, the bay in the background, Don with the perennial cup of coffee in his right hand, his left on Joe's shoulder. The smiles are genuine.

After his death, I sent a copy to his mom. I intended to send Joe one also and got his address from Grace, but could never bring myself to mail it. I wasn't sure he'd remember me after all those years. I knew Don had corresponded with him throughout his life and I did yearn to touch those lost years even at such a distance. But I think a small part of me was still jealous of the longevity of their relationship. I was glad Don kept the connection, but just as I had that weekend so many years ago, I wanted to be included.

The day after Joe left, Don was back at work at Sears. I was at loose ends and anxiously paced the house, unable to get myself to go outside. I called my parents and asked them to keep the kids another couple of days, but they had other plans. Even their arrival that afternoon did little to fill the hole in my gut. Something was very wrong and I was desperate to know what it was.

I can't recall anymore what I was looking for rooting around in what we jokingly called the "un-closet" off the master bedroom The deep set closet was intended as a second walk-in but was never finished. Lacking even a door, it became a dumping ground for boxes, out of season clothes, old books and school papers. I literally stumbled across it, a small black ledger with no identification. I absentmindedly thumbed through it, wondering which of my books it was, thumbing through the pages trying to place it in my memory.

Oh Shit. It was his. I knew Don kept a journal, but it never occurred to me he would leave it lying among my old books and papers. It wouldn't have dawned on me to go looking for it. Privacy to me was inviolate. Desperation overcame ethics, however. *What had I done? What was the matter?* My hands shook as I opened it at random and read a few pages. Angst, depression and isolation grabbed at me. Each page recorded his desperate need for me, his love for me, the depth of which apparently had shocked and rattled him. His pain was tangible. I felt miserable, like a peeping Tom, an emotional rapist. I flung the book away in disgust of my lack of character. That's when I saw it. Something had slipped from the pages. I picked it up and turned it over. It was a snapshot of an attractive young woman in a bikini on some generic beach. The girl was thinner, but I recognized her immediately as Don's "friend" from work, Beth. Even then, it took me a beat or two before it all fell together, before the key to the cognitive maps, as a psych professor might say, fell into place. The photo passed critical mass and I felt the last several months click into place, like an intricate set of dominoes set into motion. *Another woman. He was seeing another woman. What a jerk I was; it was obvious. No sex, staying out late, vague answers to innocent inquiries.*

It came back to me in a rush, how her name kept coming up all the time. I'd noticed it but been relieved he had a friend besides me. I thought it might ease the tension between us. *What a fool. Why, just last week he gone out of his way to pick a fight with me, staying out late and making sure I knew they were out drinking together.* He had even tried to tell me.

"How's your friend Beth," I asked, trying to make some noncontroversial conversation? "Did she enjoy her Bermuda vacation?"

"Yeah. She brought me back a T-shirt that says, "I'm involved," he answered. Like an addled-brained fool, I had continued chopping vegetables, "That's so sweet."

Poor Don, he must have gone nuts. I just refused to let him break it to me. Talk about thick as a brick. My concern for "Poor Don" didn't last long. *The little shit lied to me. He's having an affair at the least. What am I going to do? He doesn't love me anymore. I am abandoned.* I reeled back on my heels as if struck by a board broadside. Intense nausea gripped me and the room seemed to fade from color to black and white like a photo negative. I shook myself conscious, back to living color, but my reward was dizziness and shortness of breath. My chest was tight, the life squeezed out of my heart. I don't know how long I stood looking down at Beth's smiling image. It seemed like hours, but was likely only seconds. When I could suck in some air without gagging, I picked up the journal, slipped the photo back in and dropped it among the books, not caring if that was its original resting-place.

The next few hours were crazy, crazy in their extreme sanity and routine. Although it was early afternoon, I started cooking dinner. An elaborate meal of barbecued spare ribs, risotto, several kinds of vegetables, a mixed green salad. I cut up grapefruit to begin with and baked cornbread, going so far as to run down to the liquor store for a bottle of red wine. I never brought wine.

The kids were excited and wanted to know why we were having a party on a regular day. I told them I was just glad they were home and wanted to celebrate, a lie that turned my innards a bit. I cleaned, a real departure. I set the dining room table with the good stuff. I was out of my mind, clinging to sanity by repeating simple gestures. Immediately after my father suddenly died years later, I would also clean, do laundry and make beds, as if by enforcing extreme order you could maintain control. It's a mental delaying tactic, a buffer, to give you a chance to take it in bit by bit. Your body is somehow trying to tell you that life goes on, that we continue in the face of it all. But that knowledge fades when the force of the trauma, the reality of the loss, the panic, sets in. Numbness only lasts for a short time.

When Don walked through the door and took in the surroundings, the blood drained from his face. We sat down to eat and made it through the grapefruit without incident, making edgy small talk. As usual, the kids ate fast and wanted to get on to more interesting endeavors. I was glad and petrified when they left the table. We looked at one another for a long time. He cried first. I didn't say anything about finding Beth's photo, but he could see it was over.

"I'm seeing someone else."
"Beth?"
"Yes."
"Are you in love with her?"
"I don't know."
"Are you sleeping with her?"
"No," he paused. "That's worse isn't it?" I nodded, but I didn't believe him, even then.

"I love you," he croaked through tears.

He then went into some long explanation I didn't want to hear, about how he tried but couldn't tell me, how upset Beth was that he couldn't bring himself to come clean. He and Joe had gone to New Brunswick with Beth that Saturday night. *How humiliating. Joe had been here to see me groveling around trying to fix things that whole weekend and all the while he knew.* The humiliation brought angry tears to my eyes, the room closed in on me and I could feel the air pressing hard against my temples. Tears ran onto my plate of ribs, mixing with the pungent barbecue sauce. I had to get out, escape. I jumped up from the table, grabbed my car keys, and before Don could stop me, drove off.

I couldn't see very well because of the tears. I dashed up the parkway and ended up at Carin's house, cutting the 45-minute drive time in half. She opened the door, took one look at my face and quickly ushered me up the stairs to her bedroom. Out of the corner of my eye I could make out a living room full of women. I tried to talk but could hardly make coherent sounds through the sobs. Somehow, she caught the gist of it.

"Stay here. I'll be back in a while. I have a house full of people. Remember, this is the date of my Tupperware party."

She was in the middle of a Tupperware party. My life crashed and burned and she was sitting in her living room burping plastic containers. My timing always did suck but so did her priorities. I started to laugh, almost hysterically, but grabbed hold of myself. Carin would never forgive me if I made a scene. I picked up the bedside phone to call Don, but changed my mind. *Fuck 'em. Let him sweat for once.* I knew he'd be frantic with worry and guilt. After all, I'd jumped behind the wheel of a car crying and having had several glasses of wine. This time he was stuck with the kids and couldn't come after me, a small mercy for which I was grateful.

I lay curled up on her antique cherry four-poster, hugging my knees to my chest, rocking back and forth. Carin told me later she had checked in on me several times, petrified I was lost to catatonia. I left before she was finished with her guests, though, fed up with being put on hold once again in favor of her social obligations. Never in my life had I felt so empty, so alone.

The house was still and dark, the table was as I had left it, as I imagine dinner tables were when in Pompeii when that volcanic eruption froze time in white-hot lava. Don sat on the sofa in the dark, a cigarette in one hand, the empty bottle of wine and a glass in front of him on the cedar chest. He rose as I came in, but I brushed past him, exhausted, and went up the stairs to bed. I don't recall hitting the sheets or whether he came up to join me.

If I Laugh

He left as the azaleas were blooming. The gap between the world around me and my internal landscape was crushing. Pain would well up erratically and ambush me. My friends Natalie and Samantha were running a fishermen's café called the Galley for the summer, and I spent most of my time hanging out there, driving them crazy, I'm sure. But they knew enough to let me alone. Often, I'd walk straight back into the kitchen to wash the dishes, something I avoided at home at all costs. The kids would go off to day camp and the emptiness and quiet would close in. Then I escaped to the Galley, to the company of humans, the sounds of life. I was deep into mourning, along with a relationship a part of me had died.

Living on unemployment, I was unable to look past the hot water gushing down the industrial-sized sink, the soap bubbles climbing to the top, threatening to overflow the sink as my emotions overflowed my body. As I washed, silent tears ran down my face into the water. I didn't bother to hide or try to control them. Somehow, the elbow-high hot soapy water I felt through the rubber gloves released me. Giving a bubble bath to absurdly large pots and pans, I disappeared, and the rhythmic movement would lull me into a trance, a moving meditation. For a while time would vanish, Don would vanish, the outside world would vanish. Peace. When the chore was over I would snap violently back to my world of abandonment.

It taught me something valuable, though. Thereafter, I would use mindless, repetitive work as a passage to inner tranquillity. It usually involved some sort of cleansing, I noticed. Peacefulness was as close as a floor needing scrubbing, grout in need of attention or brass that could use a polish. It had to be something completely mindless. Cleaning out drawers or reorganizing closets may provide a sense of control and accomplishment but not the inner stillness of rote work. It's the mindless repetition. It occupies the conscious mind, anchoring it to simplicity and getting it out of the way.

I wasn't expecting him, not really. OK, so I was hoping he would put in an appearance and maybe even a bit more. It was my birthday, after all, my 30th birthday. I'd killed the day at the Galley. Nat and Sam had made me a cake, and as the fisherman came back early in the afternoon, they joined in singing Happy Birthday. My kids were sweet. Lizzie wrote me a poem and Josh drew a picture of the three of us. I worked hard at being content. But as the evening settled in so did the restlessness.

Many people would have poured themselves a few drinks, others curled up with a juicy book, maybe a mystery. But by now, alcohol was starting to scare me and, I couldn't concentrate enough to read. My eyes kept glazing over but not even tears came. Finally, I picked up a deck of cards and made myself comfortable on the couch in front of the TV. Between whatever was on the tube and the motion of my hands perhaps the night would pass relatively painlessly. In the morning, my birthday would be past, and so would the burden of celebration. By 9 p.m., I was into a pretty good run of solitaire. Switching between three-card-and-over and the official Vegas single-card version, I kept interest up and cheating to a minimum. I was feeling OK, not great, but a familiar level of numbness had set in.

The knock at the door startled me and I dropped the cards. It was him.

"Happy birthday," he said, leaning over to brush my cheek with his lips. I managed a "thank you," picked up the cards and sat back down on the couch. He took in the TV and the game of solitaire, brushed away the cards and sat down on the chest facing me. He took both my hands in his.

"You shouldn't be here like this . . . waiting."

I glanced around and realized how it looked to him. He assumed I was waiting for him. *Was I?* I was conscious only of waiting for the night to pass. I'd spent many nights—too many to count—the same way stretching back long before we met. As an adolescent I sat in the living room bay window playing solitaire for hours as I watched the cars go by, waiting for my life to start. Perhaps he was right. I was still waiting. I opened my mouth to explain but the words rang false and tinny inside my own head. I remained silent instead, relishing the touch of his hands in mine.

He wore a somber expression and his eyes were hooded in pain. As he made a determined effort to look me square in the eyes, I braced myself and tried to pull my hands away, but he held fast.

"I don't want you to wait for me, Deborah, "he said. "You are not in my future plans."

He might as well have locked his hands together and hit me full force with his body weight. I literally reeled against the sofa back. Determined not to cry anymore in front of him, I felt my eyes and face grow hot.

"You have so much to offer. It's such a waste for you to lock yourself up in this house."

As he kept talking, I nodded occasionally but had stopped listening. His voice grew smaller and smaller, as if coming from a distance, although he still sat inches from my face. Eventually, he let my hands drop. By then, I had reclaimed enough of my composure to lie.

"Not to worry, babe. I'm doing just fine."

He gave me a long look. I held his gaze, but I knew he realized I was full of shit. Regardless, he accepted my statements at face value and beat a quick exit. As soon as the door closed, I headed for the bathroom and threw up. *If he doesn't expect me to be waiting for him, what was he doing dropping by?* The retching continued until there was nothing left to give back. Weak and dizzy, I almost didn't hear the insistent rapping at the front door. *What the hell does he want, now?* It wasn't Don, though. It was Bobby, walkie-talkie in hand, squad car left running at the curb.

"You didn't think I'd forget your birthday, did ya," he said brightly.

"Thanks for stopping by, but I'm really not feelin' all that great. Must be a virus or something."

I started to close the door, but he held it open with one meaty hand.

"Yeah, and I'll betcha it's a virus carried by an Italian piss ant . . . I'll be right back. Don't even think about closing this door."

I leaned against the door jam, watching as he shut off the patrol car and spoke into the walkie-talkie. I couldn't hear what he was saying, but I didn't need to. He was giving the code for being out of the car at this location.

"Coffee on?" he said, striding past me into the kitchen.

We sat together at the counter for an hour or two, talking about anything and everything except what was on my mind. Then a call came in.

"I have to get back, Deb . . . I think maybe you should hit the sack. You look like hell."

"Well, at least you and Don can agree on something."

"Don't you dare use my name and his in the same sentence. Now go on upstairs. I'll lock up."

"I don't think I can make it up the stairs tonight. I'll just stretch out on the couch in the den."

"No way. Not on your birthday," he smiled. "Come on, I'll give ya a hand."

Bobby took my hand and led me over to the stairs, and then, straight out of *Gone With The Wind*, carried me up the stairs to my bedroom. As miserable as I was, I couldn't help grinning. I let my head fall against his chest.

"Why sir," I said in my best Scarlet O'Hara voice, "I do declare. You take my breath away."

"Don't get carried away," he announced, unceremoniously dumping me on my bed.

"Sure I can't interest you in joining me here after your shift?"

"Interesting me has never been the problem, darlin'," Bobby murmured softly in my ear. "Happy Birthday." He kissed my forehead and tucked the sheet around my body before he left.

Not long after that, I gave in to the impulse to stop by Don's Toms River apartment unannounced. I knew it was a stupid idea, that I would regret it big time, but I did it anyway. Beth answered the door. I swallowed hard. He wasn't home and she asked me in. I couldn't bring myself to cross the threshold so the unlikely pair of us rode down to Dunkin' Donuts for a cup of coffee. We talked for several hours. I was miserable, and I knew she felt badly about it. Most of my friends thought I was totally bonkers, but I couldn't work up much anger toward her. Later, I convinced myself she had done me a favor by coming along when she had.

Strangely, she didn't seem all that happy herself. I assumed she played down their life together out of polite consideration, so as not to add to my despair. After all, they were in the initial stages of a love affair, that time when your feet dance above the stones and broken glass of life. Then, the significance of her remarks blew right past my frozen brain.

"All we do is go to bars," she said. I nodded in recognition. "And he gets drunk and cries about how much he misses you and the kids."

"Really?"

"I thought it would stop when we started living together, but it hasn't."

Any relief I may have felt in his sodden displays of longing for me and the kids was washed away. They were *living* together. I struggled to maintain my composure. But what was left of my heart disintegrated right there, before the trays of glazed, powdered and filled donuts, on a stool at the counter of a pink and white, open-all-night Dunkin' Donuts.

While far from friends, we did feel connected, Beth and I, by love and heartache, by semen and soul. Down the road, we were genuinely pleased to see one another at our rare chance meetings. While eating at a steak house in Brick Township with my parents years later, I looked up at the familiar voice of our waitress to find Beth, pen poised over pad. We actually embraced like long lost friends. By then he was long gone from both our lives.

Beth was closer in size and coloring to Don's mom than me, with round, dark eyes to match his own. She was near his age and from a similar cultural background. Beth worked alongside him at Sears, and while bright was not an intellectual. Don told me once she was fearless, so he could be fearless also. And, of course there was no scar tissue—at least yet. Somewhere deep inside he also realized, I believe, that I would not accompany him down the road to full-blown alcoholism, so he found another female companion. And she took the trip with him . . . until motherhood intervened.

Being hit with the news that the two of them had set up house together didn't help bring me around. I spent hours swinging to and fro in the living room hammock, listening to Joan Baez's "Diamonds and Rust" and sobbing. I loved the hammock. I didn't mind that the kids knocked up the walls by swinging too high and too hard, or that the rope could cut into my skin and leave marks. It was my version of a rocker. Not much for insects and the like, I would spend Sunday morning or lazy afternoons swinging gently, reading and listening to music. It was calming, and being inside, I could enjoy rocking back and forth as the snow fell.

When Jeff and I married, we had no money for furniture or decorating. So I painted the wall a combination of vibrant yellow and red. It was the 70s. For furniture, we made do with our first and only upholstered purchase, that tan corduroy Castro sofa, kind of an art deco piece, and a wicker love seat and chairs. After Jeff and I were history, I hung the full-sized rope hammock across the end of the living room, looking out over the street and the water beyond.

Before the hammock period was over, I'd purchased several. We kept wearing them out. The rope knots would fray, the cord grow thin and eventually break, once sending my unsuspecting mother crashing to the floor. Lizzie and Josh would throw a blanket over it and use it as a fort. Don loved it as much as the kids. He must have said a hundred times that he would always have a hammock in his living room. I'm sure, like so many other things, he meant it at the time. That last weekend with Joe, I took a snapshot of him in the hammock. He is sitting in it sideways, like a chair, leaning back with his arms flung out perpendicular to his body. The smile on his face is peculiar, his eyes little slits. It is obvious he is high. As disturbing as the photo is, I have kept it all these years. I have a really hard time throwing out any stuff he left behind.

By the middle of August I was all cried out, at least for a while. I started applying for work and landed a job managing the china department at a store in Monmouth Mall. I knew next to nothing about the product and hated retailing, but I was out of money and desperate. By then, I realized my psych degree minus a masters or doctorate wasn't much of a ticket to gainful employment. And I had neither the focus nor funds left for more schooling. I could have gotten a marginally paying job at a nearby center for emotionally disturbed kids. But I had little left to give and couldn't bear being around any more pain. So I took the job at Hahnes for $10,500 a year and medical benefits. Getting myself together to work full time gave me something else to concentrate on, and learning a new job, being in a new environment gave me the illusion of starting a new life–for a short time, anyway.

He was paying me a visit at work, coming to the mall on the pretext of returning my prized copy of "Atlas Shrugged. " I'd had the Ayn Rand tome since I was 17, and it was underlined and annotated like many people's bibles. I was happy to get it back, but happier still to see Don again. My job was vacuous. It was impossible for me to be deeply involved with crystal goblets from Hungary and fine china from England.

Don was coming. That's all I could think about. I hadn't heard from him since my birthday and missed him more than I had admitted to myself. We exchanged the usual pleasantries in my dingy, cramped office at the back of the stockroom. It was almost 6 p.m., so we strolled over to a small bar and grill for a bite to eat. I could hardly swallow solid food, but I did down two beers rather quickly. That was enough to set me flying. Don gulped several vodkas in the same period of time, which I chalked up to nervousness on his part. After a bland but pleasant visit, I walked him to his car.

"Get in a minute," he said. And I did. The ever-present sexual tension between us, fueled by liquor erupted, evolving into one of those endless petting sessions. He pulled away at the last moment. I was hurt and relieved at the same time. It was all too much. Overwhelmed by desire I thought was at least under my control, I ran from the car. He sped away without another word.

Feeling abandoned by Don, I couldn't bring myself to break off contact with his family. It's easy to chalk it up to an effort to hang onto him, but it wasn't nearly that simple. I really cared for them and missed the warmth of his mom and siblings. So I went out of my way to see them from time to time but tried really hard not to pump for information about Don. It wasn't easy.

Grace was a more flexible person than Richard and could more easily draw a line between the situation and the person. She was only 11 years older than I and had also been a single mother for a time. So she had some appreciation for the vicissitudes of my life. I had grown to love and admire her, for her strength, resiliency and for the son she had raised. It was clear that Don adored her, which said plenty to me. She knew how to love without clinging. The very sound of her voice still brings tears of memory to my eyes. That's why it broke my heart that time I really let her down, really hurt her. I didn't do it on purpose, but I did it nonetheless.

Don had been gone at least six months and had settled into life with Beth. I opened the door one afternoon and found Nick on my doorstep, backpack and guitar in hand. He looked dejected, so I asked him in. The kids were overjoyed and jumped all over him, yanking on his pants leg to get his attention. Once they had dropped off to sleep, he and I talked.

"I've moved out, Deb. Can I stay with you guys for a little

while until I can figure out what to do? Everything's a mess. Sandy and are quits and I can't concentrate on anything, especially school, so I'm dropping out for now."

He didn't go into details and I didn't ask, but I surmised he was having some of the same problems Don had at home, only more so. It wasn't hard to understand. The baby in the family, Nick's brown hair fell past his shoulders and in many ways he was more outspoken and rebellious than his older brother had been. Taller and lankier than Don, his eyes were a deep, clear shade of blue, his grin infectious. You could tell the two were related, especially when they talked. There was something almost eerie about the matching timbre of their voices.

"I'm not so sure that dropping out of school and leaving home is the best move, kiddo," I said gently. "It's been my experience that these kinds of quick fixes almost always disintegrate and leave us more bereft than ever."

Nick shook his head from side to side. "Nah, I'll just fail all my classes if I stay in school. All I can think about is Sandy. And all my folks can do is nag me about school. Don't you do that too, please. I just need some space to catch my breath."

I sat back and thought for a minute. "OK, here's the deal. You can stay here until you get it together. But you have to call your mother right away and tell her where you are. Agreed?"

I stood by while he called Grace from the kitchen and took the phone from him when he was done. She seemed okay with it or perhaps resigned. I guessed that on some level she, too, welcomed a respite from the constant tension. At least she knew Nick was safe, I reasoned, and not living in some drug den in Asbury. I knew she trusted me to take care of him and took it to heart.

Nick hadn't been here more than 48 hours when a Don called in a snit, screaming at me on the phone.

"What the hell is going on? How could you allow such a thing? How could you do this to my mother, not to mention Nick."

Ambushed, I tried to explain. "But, Don you don't understand, I . . ."but he cut me off with a rash of obscenities and refused to speak to Nick, ranting like a jealous lover until I hung up on him. This wasn't lost on Nick, a bright perceptive lad at 17.

"He thinks there is something going on between us," he said, grinning.

"Yeah, it's kind of funny," I agreed, secretly a bit pleased. "He's awfully angry, though."

"He'll get over it."

Nick settled in and the kids were out of their mind with delight. He had no intention of fathering them, and the three of them sang songs and rolled around on the rug. Temporarily free of his perceived parental oppression at home, Nick was light hearted. Josh was very small for his age and always wanted to be tall. Nick took him outside in the yard and shot a photo while lying on the ground in front of the kid, looking up. It made Josh look like a giant, and he loved it.

I enjoyed his presence myself. The fact it bothered Don was a small bonus. Nick brought laughter back into the house. He was sweet and affectionate and the family resemblance was also comforting in an odd way. There was no way I confused the two, but it did bring Don, or a little part of him, closer. There were a few hairy moments though.

The libido of a 17-year-old male is not to be taken lightly and this one was also pining for a lost love. Watching television in the living room late one night, things almost got out of hand. There was nothing awkward or clumsy about his pass, smoothness runs in the family. I was only mildly surprised, having figured the situation too ripe with possibilities to be ignored. There he was, alone with an older woman, one who belonged to his older brother, at least in his mind. Sibling rivalry and sex is a potent combination.

What shocked me was that I began to respond. I was so hurt, so raw, and he was so tender. Thank my stars I came to before any harm was done. Pushing him away was one tough motion. But this was a boy, Don's little brother. This wasn't going to happen, period. He took it in good graces. I think he felt he'd give it a shot. I wasn't angry and was very honest with him. We talked about it for a while and it never happened again. When we would run into each other years later, we would joke about "all the sex we never had." Still, I was a little on edge after that and didn't sleep much that night, more upset with myself than him.

"Deb, I've made a decision," he announced at breakfast several days later," but you have to promise not to tell anyone." It was a promise I regretted immediately.

"I'm gonna surprise my aunt in New Mexico. If I just show up at her door, I'm sure she'll let me stay."

"Nick, you cannot fly halfway across the country without telling your mom."

"No way. If I do, she'll tell my dad and they'll stop me . . . and you promised to keep my secret."

I let the matter drop for then but continuously worked on him to change his mind. I felt awful. I didn't want to betray or hurt any of them. His parents had every right to know, but if I broke my promise I'd lose Nick's trust and we all might lose our connection with him. *What if he just took off for parts unknown?* I even considered calling Don but stopped myself. He would probably have thought it a ploy on my part and gone straight to his parents.

I managed to delay his leaving for several weeks, offering to pay him to paint my house. I had bought the paint on sale at Sears the week after the split but never had the energy to do the job, so the cans were stacked in the hallway where people tripped over them coming and going.

"OK. When I'm finished, will you drive me to the airport and see me off?"

"No, not unless you call your mother first. I will not help you do this."

Promise or no, if he hadn't been going to his mom's sister, where I knew he would be safe and that she would know immediately where he was, I would have told her. But instead, I convinced myself it was teen bluster that he would never really go. I was wrong. I came home the next week to find the kitchen half painted and a note beside the dry paint tray.

> *Deborah*
> *Well Honey, this is it! Thank you very much for helping me out. I left my shirt for you to wear when you get in a Nick mood. (It's hanging by the window.)*
> *Expect letters and I expect some from you too!*
> *I'm sorry about the kitchen. But take it as my last unfinished work. I'm about to start a new part of my life and I'm scared, and I forgot about finish the kitchen.*
> *"Good-Luck" with my big brother. I hope you catch him!!!*
> *I pray you won't be mad when I tell you this, but I took a picture of Lizzie and Josh!*
> *"I Love you and the kids!!!!!!!!!!!! (& Sandy)*
> *Love always,*
> *Nicholas DeLuca*

Blind-sided, I stared at the note. *Oh Lord, he's gone. He's really left. Shit.* It took me a few days to work up the courage to call his mother. "Grace, it's Deborah. I'd like to come by and talk to you. Is it OK?"

She agreed, but I could tell she was upset with me.

"I'm so sorry. Things just got away from me. I never really believed he would leave."

"You really hurt me," she said. "I'm furious with Nick. But I can't believe you'd do this. How could you not let me know?"

I couldn't argue; she was right. So I apologized and cried. She was generous enough to forgive me, embracing me as I left. I never quite forgave myself.

How Many Times

Even after Don and Beth were living together, he kept calling, stopping by or dropping in where I was working. Inevitably we'd end up sleeping together. "There has to be more to a relationship than sex," he'd say, after each turbulent encounter. Indeed, as if that's all it was. Even then, I knew that sex was the way he controlled me, the only way in which he felt confident in our relationship. The lovemaking, which had been tender, became rough and demanding, lacking in warmth or affection. I wanted him so badly, missed him so much, that I accepted these liaisons in motels and cars although they were a poor imitation of intimacy.

One night we ended up at a small no-name motel on Route 88, not more than a mile from my house. He knew better than to expect an invitation to my bed. It was one of the closet-sized rooms obviously intended for hourly turnover, just perfect for our needs. Don didn't notice. He was too busy throwing off my clothes and pushing me back on the bed. It was pounding and fast and furious. And that's what I felt—the pounding. I was thrown back in time to the meaningless sexual encounters of my youth. I wasn't participating, I was watching, observing his face, waiting for it to be over. As I felt the tension leave his body, his full weight fell on me and he uttered a single word, "Mine."

The bar was dark, and I stood in the doorway for a minute waiting for my eyes to adjust. It was a week before Christmas and The Cove was decorated for the season. To the usual string of tiny white lights that outlined the windows, fresh cut pine boughs had been added, and the aroma cut through the stale smell of smoke. Men at the bar looked up as I walked in. I was overdressed for the casual tavern and knew it. But I hadn't seen Don in several months so when he called, asking me to meet him for a drink, I couldn't resist the impulse to put on the dog a bit. I could always tell him I had to stop off at a holiday party later. It was Friday, after all.

I tried to ignore the stares and scanned the room, disappointed he wasn't there yet. I busied myself selecting a table with a view of the door and ordered a Black Russian. My heart raced. *Don't be so excited. It's just a holiday drink, nothing more.* But part of me, the part still playing solitaire in the living room, hoped it was more, that maybe things between him and Beth . . .

As I slipped my rabbit fur jacket off, I glanced up. Directly across from me at the bar, someone loudly struck a match to light a cigarette, holding it a moment longer than necessary in front of his face, allowing me to get a good look. It was Don. I smiled at his sense of drama as he made his way to my table, acting for all the world as if he were picking me up. Lord, I miss this playfulness of his. I felt the tension start to leave my neck.

We sat for a while, looking at each other silently, sipping our drinks.

"Man, you look gorgeous. I've really missed you."

I smiled, resisting the impulse to say how much I had missed him, too.

"Deborah, I love you," he added, caressing my face with his eyes. Then he paused and took a deep breath. "And I'm going to be married."

Caught in he act of swallowing I started to choke. Thankfully, he was so intent on getting through his little speech that he took no notice.

"Beth and I are going to Hawaii to get married and then moving to California."

"Uh huh," was all I could manage. I couldn't tell which was worse, the news of the impending nuptials or the move to the other side of the country. Panic griped me. *I'll never see him again.* He kept talking, afraid to stop.

"I'll always love you, you know. I will never love anyone the way I love you, never have another relationship like ours."

I nodded. *Big whoop*, a voice inside my head shouted. But I knew he meant it. He still couldn't bring himself to let me go all the way. Looking back, I can see how he constantly gave me mixed signals. It was impossible for me to get my bearings. He didn't want me to wait for him, didn't want to carry any guilt for ruining my life—but he didn't want me to stop loving him, either. We were driving each other loony.

"You really think 3,000 miles is far enough?" I asked with a sarcastic smile. "I suppose it will have to be, huh? If you go much further you'll start coming back . . . You told her, didn't you, about the two of us?"

He nodded; then leaned in close. "I still fantasize about you, even with Beth."

I didn't even need to close my eyes to imagine the scene of his tearful confession to Beth, of how he had continued to see me—in all my glory, so to speak. I also knew, without being told, that he'd lied to her about me, as he had to me about her, that he had downplayed the truth and sworn fidelity from then on. The distance would be easier on all of us. I didn't trust him to stay away, nor did I trust in my own strength to send him away. We finished our drinks and then two more before I had nerve to ask him my final question.

"When are you leaving?"

"In a couple of weeks."

Suddenly, I was very tired. I got up to leave and reached for my jacket. He was already on his feet and took it from my hands, holding it open for me to slip into, wrapping it and his arms around me tightly.

"Let me walk you to your car," he whispered in my ear. "Please, Deb."

The last time I saw him before he left New Jersey with Beth, we parked in a schoolyard near their apartment and talked for hours. Neither of us wanted to leave. He took my hand in his and put it on the gearshift, sliding my fingers lightly around the tip and up and down the shaft. He stopped talking. I followed his eyes and for a few long moments we didn't speak. My hand kept caressing the gearshift. He was hard and reached for me, moaning and begging me to take off my pants, intending to pull me onto his lap. I resisted and instead reached for him, bent over his lap, taking him in my mouth.

"Don't you want me inside you?" he cried plaintively. I shook my head slightly and went down on him until he came, never letting him touch me. The most he could do was stroke my hair. He was hurt, I knew, that at this our final time together, I pushed him away. It was perhaps the only time I asserted myself, the only time I had denied him what he sought. But I was in so much pain. His tenderness put me off. He wanted to really make love; I could see the love in his eyes and didn't think I could survive it.

I didn't expect to talk with him again. We had said our goodbyes. I had emptied myself of tears. In my mind, he was gone. But he wasn't done with me yet. The telephone rang late at night, the day before their scheduled departure, waking me from a restless sleep.

"Deborah, I need to tell you something, . . ."

Oh, please, don't let him say how much he loves me, not again.

"but you have to promise not to tell anyone."

"OK, I promise."

"Beth and I aren't getting married, at least not now. We're still leaving tomorrow and everything but that's all. I wanted you to know, but you can't tell anyone else."

"Oh," was all I said. I didn't understand, wasn't sure I believed it, but still my heart soared.

"And Deb,"

"What."

"don't even try to guess why I'm telling you this."

"OK."

Guess. Who had to guess? Once they left the area there would be no way of anyone knowing whether or not they tied the knot. Strictly speaking, it wasn't any of my business. So why wake me up in the middle of the night to tell me?

I didn't say a word to anyone but Carin for a long time. When I finally broke down and told Nick about the call, he produced the wedding photos and stuck them under my nose. I hated myself for getting sucked in by him again. I didn't understand how he would be so cruel. Years later, when I had the opportunity to, I didn't bother to ask. I had already figured it out. He had been stinking drunk.

PART III: MOONSHADOW

Diamonds & Rust

March 1980

It was Nick who told me about the baby that Don and Beth were expecting. I let out a sigh of relief, realizing for the first time I had been holding my breath since speaking to him several months earlier. Disregarding his mom's instructions, Nick had already called from New Mexico to let me know the pair was coming back east. Apparently, living in California was very expensive and both of them were homesick. The news was unsettling but hearing about the blessed event put me at ease. Their marriage must be solid or Don would never have consented to have a child. Beth most likely wanted to be near her own mom when she gave birth.

A few days later I ran into Don's old friend Marc. We stopped at the Back Bay for a cup of coffee, and I broke the news to him about the baby. He painted a quite different picture of Don and Beth's life together, telling me they were flat broke and had asked to stay with him and his girlfriend for a while.

"I think they're gonna have to stay with Don's folks in Seaside," he said. "A baby. Wow, what a hole he's dug for himself.'

He called on June 18, late on a Wednesday night.

"Hi, it's me."

I couldn't speak for a few seconds, but since I'd been half expecting to hear from him, I recovered rapidly. We made friendly, newsy small talk for about an hour, wished each other well and said our good-byes. About a month later, he left a message on my answering machine that he wanted to meet me at our usual place on the Point Beach boardwalk. We sat together at Jenkinsons bar while he extolled the virtues of Tanqueray gin and Reggae music, both unfamiliar to me. It was five easy hours. We drank, walked to the inlet, smoked a joint, drank some more and walked back. Both of us were pretty wasted. And while he touched me incessantly as he talked, put his arm around my shoulder and held my hand as we strolled, the desperate longing, the hunger was gone. *It's going to work*, I thought. *We are going to make it as friends, loving friends.*

"Does Beth know you're here with me?" I asked. "I really don't want anyone in your family thinking I'm out to come between the two of you, especially now that she's pregnant."

He swore she knew.

"I've told her a thousand times how much I miss you and need to talk to you."

I had my doubts. However, he must have been telling the truth for once, because less than 24 hours later he assaulted me on the telephone, screaming about my telling his mother we were making it in motels after he and Beth were living together. Of course, that was well over a year ago, long before they were married. My wounds were fresh and I did a lot of stupid things. That was one of them. Grace must have freaked out when she heard he and I had gotten together but there was no need.

I let his hysterical tirade on the phone get to me and bawled my eyes out. But I swore it would never happen again, that I was not about to take any more of his crap. Much to my surprise, this time I meant it and made not one move toward him or any member of his extended family.

My life was full enough, just busy enough not to register my loneliness. Most of my time and energy went in to keeping my financial head above water and raising the kids. There were enough men coming and going to create a nice breeze, not much more than diversions, really. Strings of affairs with men unavailable for anything permanent, which was just fine. It had taken me too long to put myself back together after Don. I was in no hurry to put my heart and soul up for grabs again.

All was quiet on the DeLuca front until early September when

I got a very disturbing call from Nick. He sounded so depressed I could barely make out what he was saying.

"Deborah, I don't know what I'm gonna do?"

"What's wrong? Are you in some kind of trouble? Are you sick?"

"No, it's nothing like that. Out of the blue Don called and told me he never wants to speak to me again," he started to cry.

"Why would he do that?"

"I don't know, honest," he sobbed. "There isn't any reason. None of my family wants anything to do with me."

This made no sense, and I was certain Nick was leaving out a significant part of the story. But I was afraid to press. I really didn't feel like getting in the middle of things again, either. Anything I did was bound to be misinterpreted. Who needed the grief?

"Listen up, kiddo, I haven't a clue what's going on in your family. With the baby almost here, everyone must be under a lot of stress. But you mother would never abandon you, never. And whatever is going on in your big brother's head, he loves you. I've given up trying to understand why he pulls this shit. For all you know, he might still be brooding about you having stayed with me for a while. We've all seen how erratic, even cruel, Don can be at times, especially when he's drunk."

"You're the only one who treats me like a human being, Deb. The only one who tries to help. Can you speak to them for me?"

"Honey, you just feel that way now because you're so upset, everything looks out of proportion. You know how much I care about you, but I'm not in a position to call down there."

I explained the situation between Don, his mother and me.

"Nick, someone in the family is sure to call you when the baby is born, and I'm certain everything will work out after that. In the meantime, please find a clinic or somebody to talk to and keep in touch with me. If you don't want to write and can't afford to call, call collect. Promise?"

"OK... I really love ya, lady."

"Back at ya, kiddo."

I had to do something. He'd never sounded so bereft. But calling Seaside had real disaster potential. I could handle talking to Grace or Richard, but what if Don—or worse yet—Beth picked up the phone. Aside from my own discomfort, I didn't want to chance upsetting her. She would be in her eighth or ninth month by now. After a day of stewing, I decided to drop Grace a note. She must have called Nick right away, because he didn't get back to me.

But a few weeks later his big brother did. "It's a little girl. I have a little girl."

"Congratulations, papa. I take it all went well."

"Yeah, Beth is good. I wish you could see her, Deb. Donna is gorgeous, one spunky little Libra."

"Donna DeLuca . . . sounds like a stage name, very musical."

"Thanks for not hanging up on me, honey. I'm really sorry about that last phone call. I was loaded. When I saw the letter you wrote mom about Nick I felt so small. You can't know how much I've missed having you in my life."

"You're right. I can't know, not from the way you've acted. And stop using booze as an excuse. It's time to grow up, pal. You have a child."

"I want to see you, to celebrate."

"No way, Jose."

"Just for coffee, at the Back Bay. I need to talk to you. Nothing in my life is working out how I planned. Please. I'll behave; I swear."

"It ain't gonna happen, babe. It pains me to say it, but your mom is right. The two of us are a volatile pair. This may come as a shock to you, but I'm not prepared to put any of us at risk, including Beth and most especially, Donna. One of us has to be the grown-up. And I guess it's gonna be me."

"All right, I get it."

Actually, he only partially "got it." He started calling me on the telephone with increasing regularity. Once every couple of weeks became once a week and then several times a week. Often the calls were late and it was obvious he had been drinking. Mostly, I listened. He told me how wretched their life had been on the West Coast, how he had never been able to go back to college as he had planned but instead worked a string of minimum wage jobs, once as a security guard at a hospital. I couldn't help but chuckle at that, the proverbial fox guarding the hen house.

In early spring he called to tell me he had a job, at the same mall where we both had once worked.

"Guess what? I'm working at JC Penney, in the automotive section. Ain't that a kick?"

A kick? Well, I wouldn't exactly call it a kick. I still had friends from my days at Sears and often stopped in to chat. I knew what was coming next.

"When you're in the area, stop in."

"Maybe."

We both knew there was no way I could be in the mall and not drop by to see him. So for months I avoided the place entirely. Then Diane called.

"Where the hell you been, girl?"

"I've been really busy, really."

"Bullshit. We've all seen him walking around here," she said. "Why don't you come down anyway and we'll do lunch. Fuck'em."

"That's what I'm afraid of."

So I shored up my resolve and met Diane the next week for a pleasant lunch at the crepe place. Afterwards, I meandered around the mall for a couple of hours pretending to myself I was shopping. Then I made my way to Pennys.

Don was standing behind the counter. His face lit up when he saw me, and I grinned in spite of myself.

"Why Ms. Gold, how kind of you to stop by."

He quickly leaned over the counter, took me by the shoulders and planted a loud kiss square on my lips. I jumped back. He grinned.

"Don't do that."

"Aw, come on, Deb, I was just kidding around."

"I just came to say hello. I'll be on my way."

"No, wait. Please. I've got a coffee break coming in about 15 minutes."

"I don't think it's a good idea, Don."

"We won't leave the mall," he raised his right hand as if taking an oath. "How safe is that? Don't worry. I swear not to let you do anything stupid."

"Gee, that's *real* comforting," I shot back. "One, *quick* cup and that's it."

We walked down to Friendlys just outside of Sears. I glanced sideways at him. He pretended not to notice how eerie it was. I pretended not to remember the horror and hurt. *This is good*, I thought, *this will help keep me from being sucked in again.* He slid into my side of the booth. I felt him along the length of my body. A faint odor of alcohol danced off him.

"Get your sweet ass on the other side or I'm outta here."

"Kill joy."

He moved but it didn't help much. Sitting opposite each other over steaming mugs of coffee was enough. He stared at me with such intensity that my face grew hot and I had to avert my eyes.

"Don't look at me like that," I snapped without thinking.

"Well that's a switch, huh," he smiled, breaking the tension. We both burst out laughing. "Seriously Deborah, when I was out in California, I must have written you 50 letters. But I couldn't bring myself to mail them because there was no way for you to write back. I ended up burning them so Beth wouldn't find'em."

He extended his open pack of cigarettes toward me, intending that I take one out and light it for him, our timeworn ritual. Don smoked Marlboros, my old brand. I would often light them for him, discovering that lighting cigarettes rather than smoking them was my greatest pleasure. I shook my head "no" and he withdrew the red-and-white box. He paused to light up.

"Aren't you going to ask me what the letters said?" He let out the smoke in a small stream.

"No. I don't have to."

"I never really left you, you know."

"The hell you didn't." I jumped up. "Look, you've blown enough smoke up my ass these past years. Even my masochism has its limits. Don't call me anymore."

I could feel his eyes on my back as I left. He didn't follow but called me half a dozen times that night. I let the machine pick-up, but he knew I was there and pleaded with me to talk to him. I reached for the receiver once, but held my ground. His voice had the same desperate quality I remembered from the first night we had spoken, before he'd even come to dinner.

I felt rotten and good at the same time. For the next few weeks I let the machine screen my calls and eventually he stopped. At least he gave up trying to get me to talk to him. But I did start getting a lot of those hang-ups, especially at bar-closing time.

Then on New Year's Eve I picked up the phone about 8 p.m., glad for the interruption in my New Year's ritual of scrubbing the kitchen floor on my hands and knees.

"Please don't hang up," his voice said.

I didn't hang up but didn't say anything, either.

"Beth and I are separated."

"I'm sorry to hear that." I heard somebody say with my voice.

We talked for a while. He had lost his job and was living in an apartment in Toms River, not far from where he and Beth had first set up housekeeping after he walked out on me. He asked about Lizzie and Josh and even inquired into my love life. It bothered me how easily we picked up our conversation, slid into old patterns, as if there had been no break in contact. It also bothered me that his voice was so pleasing to my ear.

"I'd love to chat some more but I have plans to meet some people," I lied. Not again, I told myself. He's not doing this to me again.

"Then the kids must be at your folks for the weekend or something. How about stopping by tomorrow? I don't have a car."

"I'll see how I feel when I wake up. It's gonna be a long night. Give me your phone number."

I threw the phone number into a drawer, determined not to call him back. But by late afternoon the next day I changed my mind. The aging and slightly seedy apartment complex was near the schoolyard where we had our last meeting. It took me a couple of moments before I could bring myself to knock. When he opened the door, I tried to cover my shock at the physical change. In the six months or so since I'd seen him he had grown pudgy and his face had a doughy, bloated look. He looked years older.

"Come in. Come in," he said. "It's so good you could make it."

I brushed past him and into a living room devoid of furniture, except for a TV and a couple of folding chairs. I sat around for a few hours sipping on a beer while he regaled me with stories of his life with Beth. He told me how he had encouraged her to lose weight and how she had resisted at first and then been ever so pleased with herself.

"She even made this calendar for me for Valentine's day. A girlfriend of hers took these sexy photos of her for each month of the year."

To my surprise, I laughed. "Well, you finally got what you wanted, someone who was lean and sexy *while* you were together. She sounds very creative."

He didn't mention their problems and I didn't ask. Instead, we talked about stupid stuff, like some TV chef by the name of Chef Tell whose show he thought was incredibly amusing. I flashed on a memory of him, unemployed and depressed, wasting away his days watching TV when we were together. Foreboding suddenly overwhelmed me. When he went to the john, I got up and opened the refrigerator and kitchen cabinets. They were completely bare.

"Hey," I said when he returned. "I'm getting hungry. How 'bout we go out for a bite to eat. My treat."

"Maybe some other time," he answered. "To tell you the truth, I'm kinda tired, haven't been sleeping very well. I'll give you a call in a couple of days, OK?"

I left him that day with a sinking feeling. Something was very wrong. He was different, somehow. He hadn't even given me a kiss on the cheek or a fraternal hug, not like him at all. Maybe he's just real down over the break-up and the separation from Donna, I told myself. The only true joy in his face had come when I asked how she was.

Over next week or so I found excuses to be in the area and drop off some food, canned goods, coffee and the like, nothing fancy. He was always there, always glad to see me but showed little real interest in anything. One day I had enough.

"Get your coat. You're coming with me."

I brought him home for the day. As he reacquainted himself with Lizzie and Josh, I brewed up a batch of homemade clam chowder that he devoured. It was so natural, almost as if he'd never left. Much had changed, yet things between us remained weirdly the same. I had forgotten how damn annoying it was to have every other sentence interrupted, or how I hated it when he replied "duh" to some remark I'd made. In all the grief and separation, I had also forgotten his incredible sweetness.

"When are you taking me back?" he asked after supper. "It's getting late."

"I'm not," I answered, flatly. He cocked an eyebrow. "Don't go getting any ideas. You spend too much time alone down there. I'll make up the couch."

It didn't take long for him to be spending a few days and nights a week at my place. Now I truly felt like his "only connection" to the world. The relationship was basically platonic this time around. I would go upstairs to bed alone, leaving him to the couch. Ironically, just having him around was so wonderful that it brought me face to face with the full extent of my loneliness.

A few times, when he could borrow a car from his folks, he would bring little Donna with him. She was a sweet natured child, a beauty with blond hair and huge dark eyes. Mostly, I saw her mother's face. I loved watching the two of them together, seeing the way he looked at her, the way he handled her with just the right mixture of casual tenderness. He was a natural at it, which surprised me not at all.

So when he told me that Beth had filed for divorce I prevailed upon a friend of mine, a well-known marital lawyer to represent him.

"Sid, I need a favor."

"Well, hello to you, too. What's up?"

"That guy I used to live with is going through a divorce. He's on the balls of his ass, and I want you to help him out."

"I take it you want me to do this out of the goodness of my heart."

"Oh, come on Sid. It's a real simple deal, no property or anything. It's just that he has an infant daughter, and I want to make sure he doesn't get cut out of her life just because he can't make support payments. She's filed under extreme cruelty, not no-fault, so it sounds to me like she's pretty pissed off at him. Pleeease."

"OK . . . for you. Tell him to call and make an appointment . . . So when are we going to get together again? How about meeting me for a real long lunch next Friday?"

"I'd be glad to. Just bring a notarized permission slip from your spouse."

"Point taken. You used to be a lot more fun. But not to worry, I'll take good care of your former paramour for old times sake. It is *former*, right?"

"Most definitely. Thanks, Sid."

Regardless of what I told Sid, I wasn't all that sure it would stay that way for much longer.

"Do you ever think about getting physical with me again?" Don asked one day as I dropped him back at the apartment.

"It occurs to me from time to time. I tell myself it will pass, like a gas pain."

"Very cute, Deb. I'm serious."

"I know you are, babe. We were always serious when it came to sex. I take it that it crosses your mind, also."

"From time to time," he grinned, reaching over to brush the hair out of my eyes.

We talked a lot about resuming a sexual relationship but it never came to pass, thank God. Not long after that conversation we stopped spending time together. I can't recall exactly why. But an entry in my journal on May 2 reads: *Hardly see Don anymore. My choice. We had one huge blow-up. He drinks way too much. Enough about him.*

Skating Away

June 29

... On the positive side, surprise—Don entered detox at Marlboro—out of the blue admitting to alcoholism. He called me from his folks last night and told me he's going back for a month. I hope this marks the turn around in his life.

It seems silly now, but that phone call from Don knocked me off my pins. I knew he drank heavily but had never associated the word alcoholism to his behavior. Even then, I didn't recognize the length and depth of its tentacles, how far it had reached into our life together.

"I'm so sorry for all the pain I've caused you," he said that day. It wasn't until later I learned that apologizing to those you've hurt is the first one of those twelve famous steps after copping to the addiction itself.

After wishing him well and hanging up, I experienced another of those domino sensations, like when I had discovered Beth's photo. It all went click in my mind. The divorce papers. That day I got that call from Sid.

"Deb, I thought you should know that Don just left here very upset. I advised him not to read the diary that gets filed when you claim extreme cruelty. I told him that it doesn't mean anything, but he read it anyway and freaked out. I hope he doesn't try to talk to his wife about it. I warned him not to."

"Why? What did it say?"

"You better ask him. I have a feeling you'll hear from him real soon."

But I didn't hear from him all that soon. It was more than

apparent he had stopped at a bar first. He was particularly upset about an incident in which Beth claimed he stood in full view of the neighbors, in broad daylight, and urinated on the front lawn.

"How can she do this? Why would she say such horrible stuff about me," he cried.

Even at the time, it seemed like a weird story for Beth to invent.

"Are you sure it didn't happen? Maybe you were drunk."

"It's not exactly the kind of thing I would forget."

It was clear he wasn't lying. But it was exactly the kind of thing he would forget–if he was in the throws of an alcoholic blackout. He must have been having them for quite some time, I realized with a jolt. Recently, I'd been taken aback by the number of things he didn't recall about our former relationship, shrugging it off to selective amnesia.

Within 24 hours of leaving rehab, Don was back at his parents' home and on the telephone with me. He stopped by that evening, looking better than I'd seen him in a long time, more relaxed and less puffy. He was full of stories to tell and we quickly fell into familiar habits around the kitchen counter with mugs of coffee.

As he lit one cigarette after another, he related incidents from his month at the hospital. He talked of the incredible ingenuity of alcoholics whose supply has been cut off.

"There was this one guy who kept getting drunk although his wife had emptied the house of booze," he said with a sly smile. "She went nuts trying to figure out where he was stashing it, even looking in the yard and tearing the car apart. Then one day she pushed the windshield washer button and vodka spewed forth."

At the end of the month, the hospital sponsored a picnic to demonstrate it was possible to have fun without booze. Social interaction between the sexes was encouraged, he added, but physical contact forbidden. He left me with the distinct impression he found a way around that one, though. It wasn't much of a problem until the end of the month anyway, he added almost as an afterthought.

"Your sex drive is one of the first things to go," he explained. "Alcoholics lose their passion for sex along with everything else except booze." He noticed the slight widening of my pupils and smiled.

"You thought it was you, didn't you? You thought I was angry or that you weren't desirable anymore, huh? It had nothing to do with you. All those nights I stayed downstairs it was so I could drink. You really should check out your liquor. The bottles are filled with mostly water."

I felt like I did as a child, when I slipped on eyeglasses with a new prescription for the first time. Suddenly, I could see things I never knew I was missing out on, all the rich details of my world. All the while I was blaming myself, searching for what I had done, how I had failed or disappointed him, made him angry somehow. Tossing and turning in that big bed alone, weeping. *Why was he rejecting me?* It wasn't me he was rejecting, but life. My head began spinning. It was disorienting, like walking down the street with those new glasses and over stepping curbs that seemed higher than they really are. It takes a little while for our minds to adjust to clarity.

He couldn't have known how deeply I was hurt when our lovemaking effectively ceased, although he wouldn't have been capable of caring then, either. But my ex-husband's use of sex as a weapon, of withholding physical affection, scarred me more than I imagined. And what I saw as Don's rejection brought it all back.

I stood at the front window looking out at the water, taking it all in. He came up behind and reached around my waist, pulling me firmly up against his body. I let my weight fall back against him. Our bodies had always fit together easily. My head rested on his chest. I felt his lips in my hair as we slowly rocked back and forth.

"Let me make it up to you," he purred in my ear, the tip of his tongue dancing along its rim, "just a little."

I could never have imagined it would be like that between us again, sweet and tender, wild and rough all at the same time. Yet, it was also very different. He was reclaiming a passion for life left behind in his quest for the bottle. And I was not the same uptight young matron grateful for her first orgasm. I was comfortable taking the lead and at one point we rolled around on the bed struggling for control.

"Still trying to arm wrestle me to the ground," he laughed, pinning my wrists to the bed. "Say uncle."

"Never."

"Say it," he demanded, holding me down and locking my legs together at the ankles with his legs, moving ever so slightly inside of me. "Surrender and I'll make it worth your while."

"The hell I will."

"We'll see about that," he murmured, his tongue slipping in and out of my ear. When I turned my head away, he continued to hold my wrists with one hand, freeing up the other to cup my chin. I was helpless. He ran his tongue softly over my eyes, working down to my mouth.

"Give me your tongue," he said. I pressed my lips together out of sheer stubbornness. He laughed. "It isn't gonna work, girl. Give." He kept working on my lips with his tongue until my mouth relented. Drawing my tongue out, he sucked and played with it at will. Overwhelmed, I tried several times to pull it back into the shelter of my mouth, but he simply wouldn't permit it.

"Say it," he repeated.

"I won't!"

His free hand dropped to my breast, lifting it to his mouth. I whimpered.

"Uncle," I moaned. He dropped my nipple from his mouth.

"Did you say something?" he uttered coyly.

"Uncle."

"I can't hear you," he grinned.

"Uncle, uncle a thousand times uncle . . . I give."

He rolled off to the side of my body, keeping hold of my both my wrists with one hand, pinning the leg closest to him to the bed with the side of his leg.

"You promised," I protested. "Please."

"I love it when you ask nice."

He took my other leg in his free hand, spreading my legs barely a few inches, slowly holding it farther out as his thrusts increased in depth. He refused to be rushed and by the time he'd raised my leg over his shoulder and loosened his grip on my wrists, I was begging and screaming. We came together.

"Shit woman, you have changed," he said as he lit up a cigarette. "It's a good thing the kids are heavy sleepers. When did you get so loud, not to mention talkative?"

"I seem to remember somebody urging me not to waste my life playing solitaire." I rolled over on my side. He settled in around my back but his hands were restless, running up and down my body. I felt something familiar pressing insistently up against my rear end.

"Again?" I laughed. "Is this three or four? I've lost count. Maybe I should start dropping in to AA meetings to pick up guys."

> *August 17*
> *In the category of "for old time's sake," two weeks ago, Don, fresh out of Marlboro, seduces me and heads for the hills. The sex was more than fine, but I did make him finish out the night downstairs on the couch, which went over like a lead balloon. Tough. It would have been too confusing for the kids. They aren't babies anymore and have been through enough.*
>
> *Yesterday, I stopped in at his parent's house in Seaside to say hello on my way home from work. In the midst of a short conversation in the driveway that made no sense, he abruptly claimed to be exhausted and had to go to bed, literally running away from me. He seemed stoned or could it possibly be?? Drunk? I confess to feeling kind of confused and a bit dejected.*

I never saw him again after that; never spoke to him again; never heard his voice. My last image is of him leaning over my windshield as I pulled away from the house that day, arms outstretched, his face pressed to the glass, distorted into a weird smile. Marc told me sometime later that Don had started drinking within 48 hours of leaving rehab. For all I know, he could have gone straight to a bar when he left my house the morning after our sexual reprise. At least that news gave our final meeting a kind of sick sense.

Word of him would reach me from time to time on the rare occasions I ran into one of his former friends or his family at a mall or whatever. I seem to recall being told he was working as a house painter down in Berkeley Township and living with some woman. But mostly what I heard was disturbing. Don was drinking his way through his family and friends, getting falling-down drunk at his sister's wedding. And after having exhausted the patience of all those along the Eastern seaboard he returned to the West Coast for good.

Years later, watching a St. Patrick's Day parade in Seaside Heights, I turned around to find Angela, Grace and Richard standing alongside a baby stroller. When I asked how Don was making out, Angela screwed up her face.

"He's married again to some broad he met at AA," she said. "She convinced him not to have any contact with his family."

Like an idiot, the only thing I could think of to say was, "At least he's going to AA." But inside I felt a kind of relief. *He isn't coming back.* I tried to believe he was in my past, that I had let him go. What I heard about him made me sad, I told myself, but the kind of sad you feel for an old friend. Yet, the idea of him returning to New Jersey petrified me.

Miles From Nowhere Tuesday's Dead

I must be dreaming, I thought. The ringing of the phone eventually shook me awake, and the voice in my ear had a familiar husky quality. I glanced at the clock, 7p.m.? I had dozed off on the couch, a half-open book across my ribcage. In the second I became fully aware, I felt my heart give an involuntary squeeze. *It was a DeLuca voice . . . Don's? No,* I realized a heartbeat later. *It was Nick.* His voice was strained and formal. I sat straight up.

"Is this Deborah?"

"Yes."

"Deborah Gold?"

"Yes."

"It's Nick DeLuca."

"I know. I recognize your voice. I'm so glad to hear from you. I've been meaning to call your mother."

My eyes shot over to the coffee table, where a phone book lay open to the page with "R. DeLuca" underlined. For several weeks, I had been unable to get Don out of my mind. I wanted to ask Grace how he was doing, if she knew how I might get in touch with him, but wasn't sure she would welcome the call so I kept putting it off.

"Well, she would have been happier to hear from you then."

My heart sank. I pretended not to know what was coming.

"Don is dead."

The words bounced around in my brain, ricocheting from corner to corner. *Dead? How could he be dead? He was a boy. OK, so not a boy any more but still only, what, 39? It was too late. Why* had I been such a coward? *Now I will never hear that voice, that laugh, again, never look into those eyes again. How could that be possible?*

As Nick recited the sketchy details, I found my voice and asked to speak to Grace, but his folks were talking with the funeral director. Don had been found dead in his Oakland motel room on Monday morning, but it had taken the coroner's office a day to find the family. A chambermaid discovered him slumped over in a chair alongside the bed, an empty bottle of vodka at his feet. On the adjacent night table, the telephone was half off the hook. A list of local AA meetings lay under a butt-filled ashtray near the phone.

"The coroner said he had the heart of a 70-year-old man," Nick was saying. "All that boozing and drugging finally caught up with him."

Unable to focus, I said I'd call his mom back later and hung up. I don't know how long I sat and stared at the phone. I wanted to call someone, to share the grief I felt. But there wasn't anyone who would understand. I didn't even understand. Instead, I walked around my house blindly, opening and closing drawers and doors, peering into closets. What was I looking for?

Numb, I called back and tried to talk to Grace but kept breaking into tears.

"I'm so sorry, Grace . . . I don't know what to say . . . What was he doing in a motel room in Oakland?"

"He had written to say he was starting a new job, " she answered.

"So you guys were in touch, again." I felt so stupid. It was all I could think of to say.

Decades fell away. It was the moment he walked out the door. A part of me had assumed I'd see him again, maybe as an old man. We would walk the boards and talk about how it had been, mostly the good times, and hold each other and laugh. But he was never to be an old man.

"I want to bring him home," his mother said.

So Don would return to the Jersey Shore, after all. His parents were heading out to California to bring back his ashes. The funeral would be the following Wednesday at a little Catholic church by the sea. It was the longest week of my life.

How Can I Tell You

I wish I could tell you I didn't remember that week, that week of waiting for Don's ashes to make their last journey. I wish it was a blur; but it wasn't. It was a waking nightmare. My days and nights were shot full of pain and soaked in tears. Time became viscous as I waded from the present to the past and back, like Marley's ghost, dragging chains of misery behind me.

I cried while I drove. I cried in the supermarket. I cried in the shower and at work. Tears welled up out of nowhere, without warning. Friends, family, and coworkers cast anxious sidelong glances at each other. "What's the matter with her? She's lost her grip?" And indeed, I had. I had no contact with him for well over a decade. It wasn't as if he had been ripped from my arms. But that's how it felt. The loss was immediate, raw. I was bleeding for the world to see.

I stayed home and dug out my journals, the handful of photos and love letters, long buried in an upstairs closet. I unearthed Cat Stevens tapes, unheard in a decade. I shut off the phone and immersed myself in the past, page-by-page, song-by-song. Perhaps if I let myself go all the way back, the pain would peak and subside. It didn't; it kept building. I began to fear I would be forever lost in the 1970s.

I was reminded of how Don would notice the shades of my body language, as if he needed to monitor it to understand my verbal language.

"Do you know that every time you say 'I love you' to me you shake your head 'no,'" he said one day.

I was dumfounded. Yet even after he pointed it out, I was helpless to stop. Now, I realized it was my body expressing a truth I always known deep down; that I shouldn't love him; that I didn't want to love him; that it was another *Dark and Stormy Night*, another hypnotic story going nowhere.

He wasn't above playing games with my head, either. We were finishing a quiet and unremarkable dinner at the kitchen counter one evening when I began to become increasingly agitated. I hadn't a clue why. Don took in the look on my face and burst out laughing.

"What's so damn funny?" I snapped.

"I read this article about the effects of the subtle invasion of personal space," he explained. "So I decided on a little experiment of my own."

He had been ever so slowly, almost imperceptibly, moving items on the counter closer to me to see how long it would take me to react.

"You mean you've been at this all through dinner?"

"Yup," he smiled, a decided look of triumph in his eyes.

"Well, how's this for a reaction?" I stood up, scowling, and stomped away from the table feeling foolish and assaulted at the same time. "You won't have to fear any invasion of your personal space tonight, for sure," I shrieked from the next room.

During the long torturous months of our separation, he would often make note of how I sat or moved. We met for drinks one night at Klees in Lavallette and took a small table. After about 45 minutes he pointed to my hands.

"Since you sat down, you've been holding your hands over and around the candle as if you need the warmth."

"Really?" I looked down quickly at my hands, prepared to laugh it off, but sure enough, there they were almost hugging the red glass surrounding the stubby candle. I yanked them back as if they had been burned, but he reached over took my hands in his and gently lifted them to his lips.

It was infuriating to be so transparent, to have my body betray me to him at every turn. After a while, he didn't even need to say anything. He would just pause and my eyes would follow his glance. A habit I had of nervously playing with cocktail napkins, spinning and mutilating them as we talked surfaced years later in one of his short stories.

For the first time, I could see clearly–in the black and white ink of my journals–how much of my pain was rooted in his drinking, how I often blamed myself for his irrational behavior. How blind I had been to his symptoms.

> *Sept. 21, 1976*
> *I was feeling sick all week, yet when Don called to ask me out I was glad, looking forward to relaxing and seeing a movie together. I was happy he had made the effort.*
>
> *Don arrived a little after 7 p.m. with his brother, He was in a great mood and so was I. He showed off his new shoes and put on a new album. We got ready and left without incident (rare) for a quick stop at The Cove.*
>
> *After one drink, Don suggested we skip the movie and stay there. I told him I didn't feel like spending the night in a bar, and we left for the movie about 9:15. First hint of trouble - we got to the theater and the movie playing was not the one we had come to see. I forgot to mention that Don had also neglected to bring his wallet, so he had no proof, a situation I always find humiliating but one that doesn't seem to bother him.*
>
> *He suggested we go to Asbury Park. As he had no ID and I didn't feel like bars, I assumed he meant to check the movie houses in Asbury. Maybe we could still catch a late show. I was disappointed to learn our destination was an Asbury bar. I didn't say anything because I didn't want to spoil the evening for him. It was already shot for me.*
>
> *Upon reaching Asbury, we did our usual riding around in circles for 20 minutes before Don decided on the Warehouse, a bar frequented by Frank and Warren, neither of whom I wished to run into. As he parked the car, I kept looking around for a sign that said, "Warehouse."*
>
> *"Where is this place, anyway," I asked? "All I see is a movie*

house and those guys sitting on a stoop. Is the bar inside the theater or something?"

"You are really starting to get on my nerve," he shot back, pointing to the guys, mockingly. "Like a movie theater really needs bouncers."

I took one look at his face and all the remaining life went out of mine. The price of saving the evening had become too high.

"Why don't we just go home?"

"Fine," he said, and headed back toward the car without a glance in my direction.

We rode home in silence, him anxious to be rid of me and me beyond caring. He dropped me off, picked up Nick and left without uttering a word. I was so exhausted I immediately fell into a deep sleep.

Looking back, I am struck by how uncomfortable I was all night. Aside from a perfunctory kiss in the bar, Don didn't touch me once. He didn't take my hand or even place his hand on my shoulder as we walked. When we left the car in Asbury, he walked ahead and to the extreme right of me, as if he really wasn't with me.

The result of this debacle? Unknown. I am sad and weary. I can't presume to know what Don is feeling, but I fear this is just one more proof that it's impossible to satisfy me. But I could very easily have been satisfied—with a drink, a movie, maybe a bite to eat and then home—so damn simple. How the hell do things get so complicated? Do I give up too easily or not know when to quit? Was it just time for an argument or something more? He and I have had so much together, yet lately it seems something is missing. I don't believe my feelings have changed. And he insists he still loves me. I can't put my finger on it.

Then there were his letters, most of which were written during the months we separated for the first time, the same time period as that September disaster. The sight of the familiar rounded, beautifully controlled script sliced through me.

> Dear Deborah,
> This is Sunday. I was up at 5:00 this morning. Very interesting time of day–the morning. Not very well acquainted with it. I wasn't sure what to do. Felt sort of out of place.
> I was pretty well loaded the other night on the phone. I hope I didn't upset you. Actually, I like to upset you a little. As usual, my mind seems to be working a bit erratically this morning. I miss you. I miss your mind. I was under the false impression that most people can think. It's very disheartening, or rather disappointing to find that almost no one can. I didn't know that I was bright. I just thought that my vocabulary was a bit larger than most people.
> I'm learning so many things. So many things I want to share with you. Share like I've never known how before. I wish I had known. I've been keeping myself extremely busy for the last few weeks. I haven't had a great deal of time to think. But I do feel, even through the moments that I'm missing you so much that I can taste your lipstick, that this was necessary for us. I see what we were and what we are more clearly now than I have ever seen us. I Love you madly and await the day when we can be together again. I make no promises as you would want, and I expect none. I will continue to love you until the day I expire and I'm proud of what we are and what we are doing.
> I miss the conversation a great deal, Deborah. I enjoy talking to myself but not all the time.
> Please write. I Love You,
> Don.
> PS—I have a couple of manuscripts in the mail. Keep your fingers crossed.–Me.

To my very best friend,

Deborah, I've just been lying here thinking about you for the last half-hour or so. I'm very nervous about work tomorrow. I don't know exactly why. I have been there before. You were right last night when we were talking about the books that I've been reading and why my enthusiasm wears away so quickly. I'm just maturing quickly and finding new and unusual places to hide.

Believe it or not, I've been thinking a lot about your relationship with Ryan. I am actually experiencing guilt feeling abut that whole matter. It seems to have taken me quite a while to recognize how foolish I was about the whole thing. Of course, I wasn't quite so secure in our relationship at that time (and I guess not quite as secure with myself). I'm still not sure I could handle that particular man even now, but my point is that the last thing I want is to suffocate you any more than I already have.

I don't mean only with men–or women, for that matter. (I even think I was a little bothered by Carin at one point, not too much though.) It's incredible the way that holding a pillow over your head leaves me gasping for breath. My low opinion of myself and my profound admiration for you certainly had dealt our social lives together a crippling blow. I've always been so afraid that you would meet Prince Charmin' out there that I didn't want to ever let you out of the house–and have succeeded admirably in some instances. I didn't want anyone else to see what a beautiful broad you are and, as a result never got to enjoy your company that way myself. It's been very stupid of me and I want to apologize to both of us.

I'm want to know you and love you so badly that I feel it's definitely worth the pain of getting to know me. I may even decide that I like both of us.

I'm extremely uptight. My whole body is fighting me. I'm so terribly afraid of failing that I can't get myself to write. I'm wondering now if this letter is a start or a cop-out or a letter!

Through all this I've also been wondering whether or not I'm becoming too analytical. Must be a question you ask yourself quite often.

I Love you and I trust you enough to let you see me as I am. I hope that what you see will strengthen our love and our "selves". I'm looking forward to seeing all of you that I've never been able to see before.

I give you with Great Pleasure,
Me
PS—I Love You. We make a Great Team.

Dear Deborah,
I've just reread your letter for about the fifth time and I've found it to be a bit confusing at some points, but I guess that that's always been about par for the course where you are concerned. I sometimes wonder how I'd feel if I knew you as well as I would like. ("Boring" you thought, right?) It seems I know your thoughts but seem to be missing you by a fraction here and a fraction there. Contradictions, Contradictions.

I have never felt neglected where your love or consideration are concerned. You have loved me as willingly and as full of abandon as anyone has ever loved, and strangely enough, were even more surprised by the intensity than me. I don't feel comfortable away from you although I think we both realize I never moved away from your house or your love—not really—I have just moved out of your "family". I don't think I have ever really forgiven myself for not being able to handle that situation.

Deborah, I think I'm getting winded. I'm running, even when I don't look like it. At least, I mean, I'm trying to run, to keep up. But every time I lift my head, I'm still a step behind. I know I'm not alone. I don't feel alone—just somewhere outside of your peripheral vision. Please read this the way I'm writing it. I feel that you love me and I feel as though I'm number one. But you're such a fuckin' mile ahead of everybody, and sometimes I just can't take the pace—and I hate you for being so damn metallic and so god damn sensitive. At this point we usually have a fight. And then I pout for a while until I realize that I hate you for the same reason I love you. I'm having a great deal of trouble separating the two. Or, for that matter, combining the two.

I really want you to be happy—disregard my disguise, please—you deserve it and you work harder for it than anyone else I know, or probably will ever know. I want to share it with you someday, but I just don't think I ever can. Alcohol doesn't make me happy anymore. Nor does pot or any other up or downs suddenly. How come your happiness is happier than mine? I mean even the happiness I experience without preservatives or artificial coloring.

Y'know, my reasons for saying what I said about marriage the other day were two fold. First, to let you know how much I care for you and secondly, I wondered if those strange sensations that develop in my stomach when I think it would go away when I said it. They didn't. I feel inept. I feel ridiculous. I feel lost. Strangely enough, or maybe not so strangely, the only time these feelings disappear completely is after we make up from an argument. Suddenly then, I can see for miles. Then the light dwindles.

The newness of me is gone. All my funny "young" expressions have been verbalized. I feel as though my sense of humor now just misses sense or just slides past humor. I feel as though everything I know I learned from you—you aren't a bad teacher—I just miss me, I guess. My "smooth" skin is suddenly just skin again, as it was before you let me know it was smooth. I realize I'm rambling but Damn it—I've lost my direction—or I'm beginning to find some of my own.

Deborah, you are the wildest combination of opposites I could ever imagine . . . tough and soft, and brilliant and unusually stupid, and exciting and boring and bold and shy, and so very, very sensitive and so damn Gemini . . . I don't know sometimes how you can keep your physical self together. Oh yeah, and so unobtrusive and so damn "snotty."

It's obvious that I could never be you—even if I thought I should. I've got to be a man (an adult, if you will). I'm large enough to be one now. Tables and chairs are regulation size.

I Love you more than anyone whose head I've wiggled around in, and I honestly believe that I always will. And I honestly believe we will be married someday, if everyone continues to believe you're just a marvelously intelligent, beautiful weirdo with weirdo kids. In other words, if somebody doesn't get to you first. However, I still retain enough self-esteem to realize that there aren't many men, of any age, or "speed", who could handle you at all. And even I handled you a little. I Love You.

All my Love,
Don

After reading each one, I couldn't resist pressing them to my face, as if some of his scent remained on the fading and yellowing pages of lined notebook pages.

To My Only Love and My Best Friend,

I want you to know that your love and patience and friendship has not gone unnoticed. The last couple of months have been extremely difficult for both of us, as you well know. More difficult, I think, than any we have yet encountered. And now that they're over (I hope), I find that I have never felt more loved or more confident in our relationship than I do now. This may only be a lull in the storm, of course, but I've found that having confidence in my own feelings and my own strengths is much more appealing, and indeed more desirable than just tapping into yours. My relying on your strengths has left me extremely susceptible to your weaknesses.

I don't feel that I've been an individual for quite a while. It's seems very hard sometimes to love you as I do and remain myself at the same time. You absorb me. Your needs are sometimes, oftentimes, overwhelming. And I allow you to overwhelm me. Partly because of your great need and partly because it's so very easy for me that way (not really, but it does seem easy to become part of your tremendous undertow.) Strangely enough, the last thing you really want or need is more of a wake. I say strangely because those who don't know you as I do, or as very few people do, would swear that you love it out there in front. Don't misunderstand; I'm aware you're a bit ahead of your time and a "survivor", so to speak. What I'm really trying to say is that I am aware that you want me to share in your boldness and eccentricities, not to walk and hide behind with Jeff-eyes staring and wide open.

I hope I'm being clear.

You're not easy to love all of the time or to keep up with any of the time. However, you always remain fascinating and my favorite person and friend. Your real friends are very lucky and very smart to appreciate you as they do.

Your Best Friend and most Avid Admirer,
Don

Then there was the note I found on his pillow the morning after our confrontation over Beth. Ripped from a steno pad, the script difficult to read, the pain visible.

I've just told you how Beth has made me feel and I wonder if you're thinking that it's not your responsibility—to make me feel that way—it's my own undesirable bad feeling of myself. I haven't felt that way since the first time you climaxed.

But that's really not it—I really am a man with her because there's no scars. So many scars! I can open myself up to her in a way that I can never again let you see me.

I am love and humor and fun and a leader and a winner. That's really me and I can't get it out - and you won't let me get it out. She can. She's not afraid and when I'm with her I'm not afraid—Not even of me. The me that fails so easily. The one that cringes at life and living.

I'm through losing when I can win. I Love you I Love you I miss you so much.

Regardless of what the Beatles proclaimed, however, love is not all you need nor is it all there is. There are children, bills, crumbs in bed, alcohol, drugs, friends, music and death.

The day of his funeral left me yearning for a friend to go with me. But no one offered and I couldn't bring myself to ask. I couldn't decide what to wear, as if it mattered, as if I was going to meet him for a date. I agonized over it, pulling clothes from the closet and discarding them on the floor, like some adolescent dressing for the first day of school: too severe, too frilly, too short, too long, too fat. Finally, I settled on black leggings and a black silk kimono blouse splashed with large yellow and red roses. *Yeah, he would have liked that.* I didn't think his family would care, but if they did, so what? I couldn't see Don as big into the black mourning uniform.

Yellow rose in hand, I left the house that afternoon in plenty of time, slipped *Teaser and the Firecat* into the cassette player and in some kind of stupor headed in the opposite direction. When I came to, I turned around and sped down the Garden State Parkway at break-neck speed to get there in time. And I did, just in time to make a royal ass out of myself. By then I was past caring.

Oh Very Young

A voice was droning on about peanut butter, about Don being his big brother and if Don had a peanut butter sandwich then he wanted one also. *Peanut butter? What was it about Don and peanut butter?* The voice was familiar but distant. I couldn't see. Wiping tears from my eyes with a ball of soggy tissues, I made out Nick at the podium. I had lost track of the service. I knew my sobbing was audible but couldn't stop. *Maybe if I cry hard enough, I'll wash this whole day away.* I fixed my eyes on Don's photo and concentrated on the joy in his face. Marshaling my remaining energy, I managed to quiet myself for the duration of the eulogies. After Nick, his father rose to speak. His mouth moved but I heard no sounds. I was deaf. The air inside the church was heavy, pressing against my eardrums.

The click of a tape player signaled the end. Cat Stevens again. Moonshadow. *Who chose the music? Nick?*

Moonshadow was the perfect summary for my feelings and I would imagine those of his family. Don was a moonshadow—dark, brooding, deeply romantic and ironic.

People were getting up. I tried to stand, pushing against the pressure from above I started to rise, but my knees buckled. Just as I reached for the back of a pew, someone grabbed me. Nick slipped his arm around my waist, supporting me as we left the church.

Thankfully, the cemetery was a short walk around the rear of the church. I don't think I could have driven. Nick walked between me and his wife, holding both our hands. The music followed us up the hill.

Once again, I was grateful for his touch, for the human contact. We made our way toward a newly cleared section where the cremated were interred. It was a serene spot at the top of a small slope from where you could glimpse the ocean. The last strains of the song could be heard as we gathered.

We clustered around the small box. It was almost dusk and the last hint of spring had left the air. I grasped a black shawl close to my body with my left hand, the yellow rose dangling from the right. His father was talking again. I noted a small vial in his right hand. All of a sudden, I knew exactly what he was going to say. I had heard it all before—word for word. As he spoke, the words echoed in my brain. There's this shock of recognition, of déjà vu. *I have been here before, have heard this before. But where? A dream, maybe?*

"Don loved the Jersey Shore, but then he found a place he loved even more, Monterey." His voice cracked and tears streamed down his face. "So when we went to California to bring him home, we also brought back some of Monterey."

As if watching a re-run of an almost forgotten movie, he uncorked the vial and emptied it onto the box. Silence. It was over. People started drifting away toward their cars. I couldn't bring myself to move. *That's it? They're just gonna walk away and leave him sitting there?* I longed for the closure of a Jewish funeral, to see him safely in the ground, to pick up a handful of dirt and drop it in, one last gift. When I thought everyone was some distance away, I knelt by the box and ran my hands over it gingerly, the grit of the sand contrasting with the smooth polished wood.

My mind flashed on a short story in a women's magazine I'd read years before, told from the point of view of a young girl coming to terms with the death of her beloved grandmother. She was helping her mother bury the old woman's ashes in their backyard with her hands, mixing the remains into the dirt, revulsion and astonishment—at the pieces of bone that remained intact–giving way to healing as her grandmother melts into the earth. Much to my own astonishment, that's what I wanted to do, to rip open that stupid antiseptic box, run my fingers through his ashes, carrying at least a portion of his remains, bone chips and all–maybe even those two capped front teeth–back home with me, to nourish the azaleas he had loved. I might even have left a bone chip or two tucked behind his favorite perches inside the house. *Oh, that would be rich. His family would have me carted away for sure.*

Nick knelt alongside me as I laid the rose on the box and tried to say "goodbye" but no sound came out. I couldn't say how much time passed before Nick took my hand in his and lifted me to my feet, once again coming to my rescue.

"It's time to go now, Deb," he sighed.

"I don't want to."

"It's OK. He'll be all right," he added, reading my mind. "Come back to Angela's house with the family. Just follow my truck."

At Angela's, I showed Grace the handful of photos I have of Don. One was from Josh's birthday party. Don and Frank were sitting together in the den and Frank was painting his face. Don was wearing a white, round-brimmed party hat and smoking a hash pipe, his eyes glazed. Her face clouded over with disgust. You would have thought that pot and not booze had done her son in. *Maybe it's just Frank, maybe she couldn't stand him, either.*

"I was surprised Frank wasn't at the service," I said to Grace. "The two of them were so close once. And how about Annie?"

"Frank is very sick," she replied. "We were told he's in the final stage of prostrate cancer and expected to die within weeks. He and Annie divorced a long time ago and she moved away. We couldn't find her."

So Frank's life wouldn't last much longer than Don's. I tried to mutter the expected words of regret, but "Oh" was all I managed. I'm not proud to admit I had to suppress a smile, that very same smile I had failed to surpress upon learning of his impending shotgun marriage 20 years earlier. There are times when the universe was exquisitely, albeit painfully, just.

Don's parents wasted no time in pouring themselves highballs, while Nick and Angela opted for beer. *While in Rome.* I unscrewed the cap off the bottle of beer I picked up out of the cooler on the floor. It seemed to solidify in my mouth, and I could barely swallow. After forcing down a few gulps, I left the bottle behind a cookie jar in the kitchen. *In my family, of course, we would bury ourselves in the food, I* mused, glancing through the doorway at the dining room table laden with barely touched cold cuts.

That's when it dawned on me that we were all crowded into the small kitchen. I stifled a small chuckle. Looking around and seeing all of us crammed in to one room of my house, Don often repeated Richard's cry with mock exasperation, "There are six rooms in this house. How come we always all end up in the same one?" We'd look at each other and laugh, but nobody ever got up and left. And here we all were in the same room, even though it meant some of us were leaning against the kitchen counter.

After a time, my back started aching so I moved around the downstairs, taking in the neat and sparsely furnished home Angela shared with her husband and two girls. The youngsters pulled me upstairs to show off the room they shared.

"Deborah and Uncle Don were girlfriend and boyfriend," Angela told them. I saw their young minds working to picture me as a "girlfriend."

"And your mom and I spent a lot of time playing racquetball together," I added. "I hadn't remembered how much until I read my old journals last week."

"Yeah, that we did."

"Angela, Don loved you all so much. It's such a shame he never got to know your kids. He told me once how he couldn't wait to be an uncle. And that he sometimes wished his name was Tom, so he could be called 'Uncle Tom.'"

She cocked her head and raised her right eyebrow.

"Honest, Angela, it's the truth."

"That does sound like his sense of humor," she admitted, nodding. "I just hope he knew how much we loved him."

"Sure he did," I said, but I wasn't sure if I believed it. He very well could have convinced himself that none of us wanted him, not the real him.

"And where might your bathroom be?" I asked the girls.

Combined with the day's stress, even that small amount of beer was enough to send me to in search of the bathroom. As I opened the door, I was startled to see Grace washing her hands. I jumped back.

"Oh, I'm so sorry. I'd forgotten you guys never lock the bathroom door."

As I locked the door behind her, an unwelcome image sprung to mind. It was later in the day, the day he tortured me over the vanishing $20 bill. I was up in the bedroom, surreptitiously looking for the money–still too thick to realize the truth. Without thinking, I opened the bathroom door and caught Don sitting on the can with a Playboy in one hand and his practical penis in the other.

"Oh God, I'm so sorry," I blustered. "I . . . I didn't realize . . ."

Before I could shut the door, he flashed me a look of such fury and distaste it pushed me back several feet. I still shuddered at the thought.

Washing my hands, I studied my face in the mirror. *Lord, what a mess.* My eyes were so red and swollen from crying they looked like bright green agates shot with veins of red. My close-cropped hair, windblown from the cemetery had sprouted a cowlick or two. I tried to stick the hair back down with water to no avail.

Well woman, it's time to go home, I said silently to the reflection. *It's all over.* Stepping out of the bathroom, I literally ran into Nick.

"You really do look wonderful," I said, "so grown-up. Your wife is lovely, but didn't I hear you married an older woman and had a child?" We can't help grinning at each other. "What was that you said at the service, if Don had a peanut butter sandwich, you wanted one also?"

"You heard right. Arlene and I broke up about eight years ago. She and my little boy Mike live in South Carolina now."

"It must be hard for you to be so far from him."

"I never get used to it," he nodded. We embraced, vowing to keep in touch. I doubted we would.

It was very hard to leave. Once I walked out the door, any fantasy of a connection with Don would die. I went to say goodbye to Grace, who was sitting back at the kitchen table. I knelt by her chair, taking her hands in mine.

"I just can't believe he's no longer in this world," I said, my eyes misting over. "This sounds really weird, but I'm going to miss him a lot."

"He was so sick, Deborah. This was his second heart attack, you know."

"I had no idea."

We hugged, and she promised to mail me two short stories he had once sent her, along with a copy of the photo of him from the church.

I couldn't bring myself to return to the cemetery for six months, until Yom Kippur. Even then, I was still not reconciled to his being stuck in that box, probably surrounded by cement, divorced from the earth. I ran my fingers around the ground, its wound still raw from the placement of the black marble stone, pushing my fingers down along the side as if I could somehow touch him.

Morning Has Broken

Two years later

The ringing would not stop, no matter how hard my mind stretched to incorporate the jarring sound into my dream. As I flailed around in the blackness for the offending instrument, my eyes found the red glow of the clock: 3:02. *Oh, shit.* My heart seized. *The kids, did something happen?* I pressed the receiver to the ear pointing toward the ceiling.

"Hello," I blurted out with a nervous edge.

Nothing. Not a sound. Not a breath. *Oh, great.* Relief tempered my annoyance.

"Hello," I repeated, waiting a few seconds. "Suit yourself," I snorted, dropping the receiver back into the cradle, drifting back beyond consciousness.

Ring. Ring.

Not again. More awake this time. The clock announced 3:09. *Joy. Some drunk probably thinks he's calling home.* I picked up the phone to the same non-response.

"Wrong number," I snapped, slamming the telephone down.

This time sleep is harder to retrieve. The third time the phone rang, I didn't bother to answer. I just disconnected the earpiece and left it off the hook. By now, it was almost 3:30, and I was wide-awake, fuming. After a quick trip to the john in the chill, I climbed back under the quilt, shivering. I started to drift away, then bolted straight up in bed.

Oh, shit. How could I have forgotten?

Jumping out of bed, I stubbed my toe on the night table. *God, damn it!* I fished around in the dark for my robe, and pulling it tight against my quivering body headed to the spare bedroom closet. When my eyes adjusted to the glare of the bare bulb, I dug through years of accumulated junk, discarded clothes, boxes of check stubs and bank statements. In an old shoebox at the back of the top shelf I found them—my old journals.

I carried the box to the old easy chair by the window and rifled through them, peeling back two years' worth of my life, layer by layer. I flipped through the months, trying not to get caught in the recorded dead remnants until I reached the last week in March 1995.

That's when it started, the phone calls. Two or three times a week around 3 a.m. It was always the same. My sleep was interrupted by the ringing and haunted by the silence on the other end, no heavy breathing, no obscenities. After a short time, I would have welcomed either. I thought of turning off the phone, but I worried about missing a critical call from my aging parents. Trapped by the person on the other end, I felt assaulted, vulnerable and furious.

As I slowly turned the pages, I noted how much I had written about Don in those weeks, how much I had wanted to hear his voice, how I had looked up his mother's phone number, how he had died before I followed through. *Why hadn't I put it together before?* I flipped to April, and read how the caller had been unusually persistent one night, calling back three times. By the last call, I was out of patience and ranting.

"If you don't stop harassing me I'm going to call the police and have a tracer put on the phone."

I was just about to slam the receiver down, when I heard the sound of a match strike followed by a quick intake of breath—a cigarette being lit. Something caught in my throat, overwhelming me with a choking sense of desolation far beyond loneliness. My anger vaporized.

"Listen. Since I'm wide-awake anyway, why don't we chat for a little bit," I cooed softly. "You keep calling so there must be something you'd like to say."

For the tiniest part of a second I thought the caller would

speak. I waited. Nothing except an occasional audible breath. I had this vision of a male, sitting in a room lit only by the glowing ember of a diminishing cigarette. Patient loneliness.

"OK then. How about I talk... or better yet, read something? It can help to listen to a live voice sometimes."

I switched on the bedside lamp and rummaged through the books piled on the night table, babbling away at anything that came to mind. Suddenly, I was afraid he would hang up. I almost started reciting, "It was a dark and stormy night..." before my hand landed on Walt Whitman's "Leaves of Grass." A gift from Don decades ago, it was a tattered paperback I couldn't bring myself to toss. Half of Whitman's face was gone, along with the "L" from Leaves and "Gr" from Grass leaving "eaves of ass," which always made me smile. I opened the book at random and read without thinking. Naturally, the book fell open to well-read passages, evoking ghosts of emotion for which I was ill prepared. I hesitated, my voice wavering for a moment before pressing on, committing to the task at hand.

> *Whoever you are, I fear you are walking the walks of dreams,*
> *I fear these supposed realities are to melt from under your feet and hands,*
> *Even now your features, joys, speech, house, trade, manners, troubles, follies, costume, crimes, dissipate away from you,*
> *Your true soul and body appear before me,*
> *They stand forth out of affairs, out of commerce, shops, work, farms, clothes, the house, buying, selling, eating, drinking suffering, dying.*

I felt the words, my voice, being sucked over the phone line, as if inhaled with the cigarette smoke, giving me impetus to continue.

> *Whoever you are, now I place my hand upon you, that you be my poem,*
> *I whisper with my lips close to your ear,*
> *I have loved many women and men, but I love none better than you.*

O I have been dilatory and dumb,
I should have made my way straight to you long ago,
I should have blabb'd nothing but you, I should have chanted
  nothing but you.

I will leave all and come and make the hymns of you,
None has understood you, but I understand you,
None has done justice to you, you have not done justice to your-
  self,
None but has found you imperfect, I only find no imperfection
  in you,
None but would subordinate you, I only am he who will never
  consent to subordinate you,
I only am he who places over you no master, owner, better, God,
  beyond what waits intrinsically in yourself.

 I sense a growing calm from the other end, like reading a story to a child awakened from a nightmare. Glancing up at the clock, I'm shocked to find it reads 4:17. My energy exhausted, I pause.
 "I'm going to have to hang-up. I have early appointments on Monday and I need to catch a few hours."
 Still no reply.
 "Well, goodnight then," I murmured and softly laid the phone down, against a growing desire to stay connected. I sat staring at it for some minutes, fighting the urge to pick it up again to see if he was still on the line. Moments later, I fell into a deep sleep and awoke strangely energized.
 The following Tuesday evening, Nick's call delivered the news of Don's death. Several weeks later, I noticed the calls had stopped. It was oddly disappointing but I assumed I provided more human contact than the caller was prepared to accept. It never occurred to me the two events might be connected. *Was it just coincidence?* Nick said Don died "sometime after midnight Sunday, in the early hours of Monday," the same night I was doing that telephone monologue. *It was too much.* The shock of the news, the delay in

finding out must have pushed it from my consciousness. *It made sense.* The phone was half off the hook, Nick said, as if Don had been trying to call for help. But what if he had been trying to hang up? What if he had turned to me in those last weeks, those last minutes?

Of course, I could never prove it with objective certainty. Life is more than capable of extraordinary synchronicity. But something deep inside me cracked open and I knew, without a doubt, it was true. I was awash in joy, weightless. He hadn't forgotten me, hadn't forgotten us. Until that very moment, I didn't realized how my need to know that prevented me from completing my mourning. Even reading the short stories his mom sent me after he had died didn't put my fears to rest.

As I read his short stories, he was there, sitting next to me again at the butcher-block kitchen counter, on the black vinyl and chrome director's stools. I heard his voice in my ear, his breath and the cadence of his voice. I recognized names, places and conversations torn from our life together. Still, I feared I was merely seeing what I needed to see, a product of some neurotic fantasy perhaps?

In the story about a young man dying of AIDS who returned home to the Jersey Shore, Don used Josh's name for a small child. Josh was a grown man by then, at least chronologically. But to Don he was forever three. Just as Don to me was forever 19, far from the sick, wounded 39-year-old whose heart could take no more abuse. The sight of Josh's name knocked the wind out of me, and I gasped for breath. He still thought about Josh all those years later. Did that mean he still thought about me, about us?

At Angela's house after the funeral, I craved asking if he ever had inquired after me in any of his letters, but I was afraid. Later, as I was leaving, I pulled Nick aside.

"Thanks for calling me when your brother died. I'm sure no one else would have thought of me after all this time."

His eyes widened. "That's not true. You meant so much to him that your name came up right away. We all stood there looking at one another and I said I'd call you." Nick will never know how much it meant to hear those words, not: He meant so much to you—which was agonizingly obvious—but, you were so important to him.

Now, two years later, I finally believed it. I had always thought of our relationship as a small part of his brief life. But this wasn't so. Our time occupied a significant part of the best years of his life. Shortly after our relationship ended, his world began to unravel. He abandoned his infant daughter and his own family didn't see him, either, for the final 14 years. I suspected he couldn't stand to see the disappointment in their eyes so he stayed away.

I wanted to believe he couldn't even handle writing to me, which was probably for the best. While he breathed anywhere in this world, he was so dangerous to me that I resisted any reminders. After he died, after he could no longer reach back and reclaim my soul, only then could I invite him back in. I never could have stood close to his memory while he lived, so afraid was I of being burned.

Putting the journals aside, I canceled my morning appointments and headed to the cemetery. As always, I caressed the black marble lightly with my fingertips, laid down a yellow rose and a smooth pebble. But this time, I sat cross-legged alongside the stone for a while and read aloud from "Leaves of Grass," which opened to just the right page.

For once, there were no tears.

EPILOGUE:
Life's a Love Song

Much to my astonishment, Don loved my writing. After we'd been together a few months, I screwed up my courage and handed him a slim notebook of poetry, almost all of it written in the aftermath of my failing marriage.

"Wanna read some painfully direct poetry?" I asked.

He sat at the kitchen counter reading with intensity and was silent for some time afterward, smoking a cigarette. "This is really good. Good enough for you to write for 30 minutes everyday."

"Oh, yeah right," I laughed, waiting for the punch line, the zinger that never came.

"I'm serious," he added, earnestly, taking a long sip from the ever-present cup of coffee.

But it was hard for me to take to heart. I had no vision of myself as a writer, no idea I could ever do so. I was pleased, very pleased, he respected my efforts, but he was the writer, not me. I was the clinical psychologist to be. Except for sporadic diary entries, I wrote only when forced to, papers and theses. One of my college professors had pulled me aside once and told me that I "got more into a paragraph than anyone he ever saw," hinting at some writing ability, but I sloughed it off. Don's opinion mattered, though. It was his opinion that always mattered, for good and ill. Yet in all our time together, he refused to see that.

Ironically enough, this turned out to be his most potent gift to me. But it was years before I recognized it. He gave me the writing life, set my feet along the path to its doorway. He took me seriously as a writer long before I did.

When I tripped and stumbled into journalism at the Bay Harbor News, a tiny weekly paper, he was still on the fringes of my life, having just returned from the West Coast with Beth. I'll never know if he learned the extent of my success in later years on a large daily, or that I had my own Sunday column in the last years of his life. How hard would it have been for him to see me make a living from writing? Could we have shared it? I don't know. But I wish I'd have had the chance, at the very least, to thank him. For without him, I never would have found myself as a writer.

If he had known of my success, he would have battled a mixture of delight and jealousy, I wager. And he would have eaten himself up inside for feeling envy at my success in his field. He identified himself so early and so consistently as a writer, that his family eulogized him as such, although he left behind, to my knowledge, only those two short stories.

The journals that I'm sure he continued to keep did not surface among his effects. I know because it was one of the first questions I asked his mother upon learning he was gone. She surmised they were destroyed in a car fire shortly before his death. For a short time, I entertained the fantasy of heading out west, looking up his last ex-wife and trying to trace his last few years, like a character in a TV movie. Instead, I've grown content with what he's left behind.

I don't mean his cylinder-shaped ashtray of cobalt blue glass, actually the lens of a running light off a boat; or his favorite narrow, cream colored coffee mug painted with birds and butterflies, now with a chipped rim; or even the small piece of driftwood he brought with him when he moved in, on which a neighbor lady had painted a purple butterfly.

As I rush out the front door on an errand, I glance up and see him standing arm in arm with Joe across the street, coffee mug in hand, posing for that photo; out of the corner of my eye, I glimpse him by the stereo, arm outstretched, offering me a dance. In that nanosecond before I drop into sleep, I feel his breath on my neck and his warmth settle in around my body. And when I sit down to write, I sense his presence looking over my shoulder, murmuring in my ear.

"I never really left you, you know."

-end-

BVG